"As [the narrator's] vivid imaginary world fuses with reality this deceptively ethereal novel advances toward a dark and startling finale." —*Wall Street Journal*

"A quick, riveting read."
—*World Literature Today*

"Spectacularly surreal and cerebral."
—*Asymptote Journal*

"Uproarious and unnerving." —*Thrillist*

"Hilarious and unique." —*Crime Reads*

"Equal parts psychotic, suspenseful, and tenderly funny." —**TorNightfire.com**

"Part surreal comedy, part dark parable, Millás's wild work brings readers face to face with the mundane facets of middle-class suburban life. . . . A page-turner of the strangest order, Millás's debut stuns and entrances. It's impossible to put down."
—*Publishers Weekly* (**starred review**)

LET NO ONE SLEEP

LET NO ONE SLEEP

JUAN JOSÉ MILLÁS

TRANSLATED FROM THE SPANISH
BY THOMAS BUNSTEAD

Bellevue Literary Press
New York

First published in the United States in 2022
by Bellevue Literary Press, New York

For information, contact:
Bellevue Literary Press
90 Broad Street
Suite 2100
New York, NY 10004
www.blpress.org

This is a work of fiction. Characters, organizations, events, and places (even those that are actual) are either products of the author's imagination or are used fictitiously.

Library of Congress Cataloging-in-Publication Data
Names: Millás García, Juan José, author. | Bunstead, Thomas,
    translator.
Title: Let no one sleep / Juan José Millás ; translated from the Spanish
    by Thomas Bunstead.
Other titles: Que nadie duerma. English
Description: First edition. | New York : Bellevue Literary Press, 2022.
Identifiers: LCCN 2021033508 | ISBN 9781942658931 (paperback ; acid-free
    paper) | ISBN 9781942658948 (epub)
Subjects: LCGFT: Novels.
Classification: LCC PQ6663.I46 Q8213 2022 | DDC 863/.64--dc23
LC record available at https://lccn.loc.gov/2021033508

Bellevue Literary Press would like to thank all its generous donors—individuals and foundations—for their support.

 This project is supported in part by an award from the National Endowment for the Arts.

 This publication is made possible by the New York State Council on the Arts with the support of the Office of the Governor and the New York State Legislature.

AC/E
ACCIÓN CULTURAL
ESPAÑOLA
Support for the translation of this book was provided by Acción Cultural Española, AC/E.

Book design and composition by Mulberry Tree Press, Inc.

Bellevue Literary Press is committed to ecological stewardship in our book production practices, working to reduce our impact on the natural environment.

♾ This book is printed on acid-free paper.

Manufactured in the United States of America

First Edition

10   9   8   7   6   5   4   3   2   1
paperback ISBN: 978-1-942658-93-1
ebook ISBN: 978-1-942658-94-8

PART ONE

1

SEEING HERSELF IN THE MIRROR, Lucía said, That fat woman is me.

This was not said insultingly; she wasn't being mean to herself. She, after all, was pretend thin rather than fat. So her mother had said when she was a girl, while brushing her hair after getting her out of the bath one day, "Look at your thighs. You're pretend thin, like most wading birds are."

In bed that night, the girl puzzled over the contradiction. Why did she look thin if she was actually fat? She was to spend the next several days searching for pictures of wading birds in books, then checking her thighs, and throughout the rest of her life she monitored herself obsessively, worried that her body would eventually give her away. But she made it through the rest of childhood and adolescence without the physical changes inherent in that transition doing anything to alter her mother's pronouncement. At no point did the subtle proportions of the wading bird desert her, and these, as she came to see in time, had the effect of blurring the line between abundance and nimbleness.

At the place where Lucía worked, there was a pathologically obese woman who died upon suddenly losing weight. To begin with, everyone put it down to how fat she had been, but then they put it down to how slim she had become. Her death confirmed people's suspicions, whatever they were, given they were impossible to substantiate either way. The day after she died, the company, an app-development firm that also installed, configured, and maintained IT systems, filed fraudulently for bankruptcy and shut down.

The world was full of programmers younger and better equipped than Lucía, and now the thought of her work prospects produced a physical unease in her, which grew more intense as she left the company building and hailed a taxi—her car was at the mechanic's. She had a cardboard box full of her belongings, like good-bye moments in movies. These were:

- a snail shell from the beach that she used as a paperweight

- a ceramic cup and a box of green-tea bags

- a Spanish-English dictionary

- a dictionary of synonyms and antonyms

- a toothbrush and a tube of toothpaste

- a jar of moisturizer

- a box of tampons

- a notebook she used for working out algorithms

- a pair of thick wool socks for when the heating was down low or the air-conditioning up high

- a nail-cutting kit: scissors, file, and cuticle scissors

- a toilet roll and two packets of Kleenex

- a packet of energy bars

- a packet of disposable paper panties

The taxi driver turned out to be a programmer as well; when his company folded, he had been unable to find work again in the sector.

"With the payout and some savings," he told Lucía, "I bought myself a taxi license, and now I'm my own boss."

"And you make enough money?" she asked.

"There's the initial outlay to cover, but then, yes, if you put in the hours, you can live off it. In spite of Uber and Cabify, all that lot. But you do have to enjoy it. I love going around all day, meeting new people, listening in as they chat away in the backseat. You get into all kinds of scrapes. Plus, I imagine I'm in a different city every day. New York, Delhi, Mexico . . ."

"Which city are you in today?" Lucía asked.

"Today—Madrid."

"But you don't need to imagine that; we're in Madrid."

"But my thing is that I need to *convince* myself." He held up a self-hypnosis book he had on the passenger's seat. "It's like when you succeed in imagining what you're doing and doing what you're imagining, all at the same time, the anxiety in your life goes away. I used to be a really anxious person, but I dealt with it and now I'm able to be in Madrid when I'm in Madrid."

"Right," said Lucía.

"And when you manage to get mind and body in the same place, reality takes on this extraordinary glow. Believe me."

"Like when you imagine you're making a tortilla while you're making a tortilla," she said, her irony lost on the man.

"Exactly. Or like imagining you're having sex at the same time as actually having sex."

She said nothing to this; it had to be a come-on. She caught the man's eye in the rearview mirror, and though he was nice-looking enough, she thought it wasn't the moment.

It was midmorning when she arrived at her apartment. She put the cardboard box down by the front door. Rosi, who came and did three hours of cleaning twice a week, was doing the vacuuming. Lucía asked her to take a seat before telling her she was going to have to let her go, at least until she herself found another job. Rosi coolly heard her out and, after they'd settled up, left the vacuum cleaner where it stood, without unplugging it. Before going out, she took the apartment keys from her pocket and flung them onto the sofa, though they bounced off and landed on the floor near Lucía's feet. Lucía hadn't expected thanks, but she'd anticipated at least a rundown of the chores.

The dishes Lucía had left in the sink had been washed up. She moved the vacuum cleaner aside with her foot, took two steps, and stopped in the middle of the kitchen–living room. She stood doing nothing, feeling afraid, as though having found herself in an apartment that wasn't her own. And really, at that hour of the morning, it wasn't. She took her shoes off and went through to the bedroom to see if the bed had been made. The atmosphere felt slightly sinister to her; the building was completely silent, like everyone had fled following a nuclear attack warning.

The bed had also been made.

She went into the bathroom, looked at herself in the mirror, and it was then that she said, not in an insulting way, That fat woman is me.

Then opera music started to play. At first, she thought it was inside her head, but then she realized it was coming through the air vent above the bath. She didn't like opera and wasn't in general very musically attuned, but there was something about this—a sort of eavesdropping, without knowing where the music was coming from—that hit her like a truck. She owned a CD of Maria Callas arias that had come free with a Sunday supplement sometime before. She had put it on one day, simply for something to do, but turned it off after a couple of minutes because it made her feel uneasy. The aria coming through the air vent was the first one from that CD; she recognized it straightaway from the familiar unease it produced. Now, however, sitting on the edge of the bidet and listening, she was in rapture. Before long, idiotic tears were flowing down her cheeks.

"Something's going to happen," she said.

This was a phrase she had spoken thousands of times in her life, though it did not, in general, precede anything happening. She had gotten it from her mother, who would sometimes stop mid-action and say, "Something's going to happen," followed by a vacant look coming over her. Then, since nothing happened (nothing visible at least), she would go the rest of the way down the stairs, or finish brushing her hair, or whatever it was she had been doing before the sudden stoppage. Lucía had inherited that sense of some vague but threatening event being constantly just around the corner.

But there had been one occasion, on the day of her tenth birthday, to be precise, when something had happened. Since it was a Sunday, the girl had run into her parents' bedroom the moment she woke up and asked for her present, about which the only clue she'd been given was that it was a surprise. While her father got out of bed to fetch it, her mother sat up and said, "Something's going to happen."

At that moment, Lucía's father came back in with a bird in a cage. Its beak looked disproportionately long and its feathers were so black as to look blue. Its head shifted nervously from side to side, as though it was looking around for someone it knew, first with the left eye, then with the right. At the girl's ambivalent look, her father said, "It was your mother's idea."

Her mother then went over to the cage, pursed her lips, and made a sort of click with her tongue, which seemed to soothe the creature.

"It's called Calaf," she said. "It's come all the way from China."

"Can I pet it?" Lucía asked.

"Once it gets to know you."

There was a party for the girl in the afternoon, with family and various school friends invited. The plan had been to celebrate out in the garden, but it had rained in the night and the grass was wet. Everyone was, therefore, inside, in the kitchen, where the girl had just blown out her ten candles and her father was handing out slices of cake to the children. It was then that Lucía noticed her mother had disappeared, and she went to look for her in the living room. There was no sight of her, but something prompted Lucía to look out into the garden, where, she found, her mother was crouching down to pee. The scene made the girl uncomfortable, though she explained it away, imagining that perhaps the downstairs bathroom had been occupied.

She watched as her mother lifted her skirt, pulled down her panties, and crouched down, only for a blackbird to then drop from the sky like a missile, crashing beak-first into her head. Lucía heard the sound of the bird's neck breaking on impact, and the crunch of her mother's skull. Both mother and bird fell to the ground, unconscious or dead. Lucía was rooted to the spot, unable to move or cry out, as always tended to be her way when it came to any moment of conflict in her life.

Her father, having noticed mother and daughter missing, came in and, seeing the girl staring in horror out of the window, opened the door and went into the garden. In the time it took for him to find Lucía's mother, and without his being able to see—the mother had ducked down to pee behind some shrubs—Lucía saw a kind of soap bubble with smoke suspended inside it emerge from the bird's beak before entering her mother's mouth, squeezing its way in between her lips. With that, she came around. Lucía's father found her, and Lucía saw her trying to explain what had happened, pointing now to her head, which was bleeding profusely, and then to the dead bird.

With the help of Lucía's father, she pulled her panties up and, leaning on him, returned inside. One of Lucía's uncles, a doctor, was there, and he, examining the wound, said it needed stitches.

"Maybe a tetanus shot, too," he said.

Her mother and father hurried off to the hospital and the party continued under the supervision of the remaining adults. Lucía pretended to be having a good time, and she even made an effort to do so, but the events of earlier on meant she found it hard to throw herself into the proceedings fully.

Her parents came back three or four hours later, by which time all of Lucía's friends had been picked up. Her mother had a bandage on her head, with a shaved patch around it. Part of her head had been shaved. But she felt fine, she assured them, in spite of the ten stitches—ten, the age Lucía now was.

Her mother and father had a drink, everyone saying what a crazy thing it was to have happened, and her father then suggested they go out and take a look at the dead bird. It was dark by this time and there were no outside lights, so they took the powerful flashlight with them from the garage. Lucía thought the bird looked like Calaf, the bird she'd been given as a birthday present.

"It's a giant blackbird," said her father.

Lucía's uncle, the doctor, wasn't so sure. Though the orange beak looked like a blackbird's, the creature was closer in size to a crow. Both thought the best thing would be to put it in a plastic bag and then in the trash. Her mother, though, said they ought to bury it where it lay, and nobody dared argue. So Lucía's father brought a shovel from the garage, dug a grave, and dropped the bird inside before covering it over with soil. The girl's uncle said his good-byes and then it was time for Lucía to go to bed.

Before she got into bed, she spent several minutes observing Calaf, sliding a pencil in between the bars of the cage, which the creature came over and pecked. She'd been told that, with patience, she could teach it to speak.

"Something . . . is . . . going . . . to . . . happen," she said, enunciating slowly.

The bird responded with a click of its beak, similar to the tongue click with which her mother had calmed it earlier in the day.

She was in bed, and about to close her eyes, when her mother came in and asked if she liked her present.

"I quite like it," said the girl.

Her mother said she was sorry about what had happened, to which Lucía said nothing. Part of her wanted to confess to having seen the whole thing, but she also understood that it wasn't really her mother she wanted to confess to, but, rather, the bird that had dropped out of the sky and hit her. She decided not to say anything; she didn't want people to think she was gaga. She fell asleep trying to convince herself that she had dreamed the whole thing up.

Not long afterward, Lucía's mother disappeared from the house.

"She's in the hospital," her father told her.

"She's in the hospital," repeated the rest of the family, as though going to the hospital was something everyone did at some point.

Several months passed, and when her mother came back, she was thin, pale, and silent, and her eyes wandered, as though she were seeing things invisible to the rest of humankind. Lucía and her father helped her into bed, where she stayed until her death. Her nose, of the kind people call "aquiline"—a feature Lucía inherited—had become even more hooked, even more beaklike. She died before her daughter's eleventh birthday came around, and in her presence.

"Something's going to happen," the dying woman had said, eyes skittering across the ceiling and walls, as though a swallow had just flown in through the open window. Lucía, following where her mother was looking, thought she saw a bird-size shadow cross the room.

Her mother smiled and let out a faint rattling exhalation, and her eyes fell shut. The girl knew full well she was dead, but she pretended she didn't, and told only Calaf, her birthday present, with whom she had by now established an intense friendship.

Something's going to happen.

The phrase occasionally manifested in Lucía's head like a ghost in a hallway, and with the exact same intonation as when her mother said it. Whenever it did so, a shadow in the shape of a bird flew swiftly across her mind.

LUCÍA AND HER COLLEAGUES attended the funeral of the pathologically obese woman as a way of supporting the family. As the coffin was lowered into the grave, a large bird came and flapped around above the heads of the relatives, and Lucía was reminded that the following day was the anniversary of her mother's death. The news of the company's closure, brought about due to a bankruptcy claim that turned out to be fraudulent on the part of the owner (who turned out to be a crook), she decided to accept, as though it were a gift in disguise.

Something's going to happen, she thought, and two seconds later Maria Callas's voice was drifting in through the bathroom air vent.

And she, sitting on the edge of the bidet, wept like an idiot because of musical manifestation that, had she herself decided to put it on, would have struck her as nothing but a horrible grating noise.

2

GIVEN THAT SOUND, like smoke, tends to rise, she guessed that the music was coming from the apartment below, on the third floor, but, even though she had been in the building for seven years, she couldn't bring herself to go and speak to the person living there. When her father died, she had sold the family home, which had been on the outskirts of the city and boasted a garden, and bought this two-room apartment on the corner of Canillas and Cartagena. And she had some money left over, which she put into savings; money was something that gave her a feeling of security.

She had never met any of her neighbors. It was the kind of place where people didn't stay long, given that the apartments, almost all of which were rentals, were occupied by recent divorcées or people only in Madrid temporarily. There were students, too; they would move in at the beginning of the academic year, October, and be gone in June. For some time, Lucía had also been seeing tourists in the elevator; they must have rented the apartments online for a few days at a time.

The transience of the building's inhabitants was the very thing that had sold her on it; she had never been able to stand neighborly interactions. The only constant was the super, a Polish man, who, able to turn his hand to fixing plugs and cisterns alike, saw to the upkeep of the building as well as manning the super's office. He showed up in the morning and disappeared at night, and let everyone have his number in case of any after-hours emergencies.

Lucía did not know how long she'd been sitting listening to the music coming through the air vent, because she had entered a dreamlike state, one in which her future career had also been revealed to her: She saw herself driving a taxi around the streets of Madrid. She visualized the city as seen from a driver's seat, with her continuously zooming in on people and buildings, swinging to the left and then, for no apparent reason, to the right. She liked driving, always had. It was not something she found tiring. She sometimes went out in the car for hours, covering distances of 250 or 300 miles, for the sheer pleasure of that six or seven hours in nobody's company but her own, letting the motorway unfold before her as she turned this or that over in her mind.

In her mind, as she drove this taxi, the opera music she could hear in the bathroom was playing; she imagined it coming from the car stereo and not the downstairs apartment. The melody both broke her heart and plunged her deeper into the day-dream. She went on with it, imagining stopping to pick up a passenger, a man of forty-five or fifty, well-dressed, polite, wearing expensive cologne, which melded with her own perfume, intermingling like the smoke from a pair of sweet-smelling cigarettes. That invisible dance between the two fragrances, with Maria Callas's voice increasing the aromatic tension, sent a shudder through her entire body.

"Do you like opera?" the man asked.

"I'd like to like it," she replied, and she meant it.

It seemed more seductive to present this combination of inadequacy and ambition, given the position of superiority it put him in—always a turn-on for men. The reverie had become extraordinarily real at the moment the music stopped, suddenly pitching Lucía back into the bathroom. Her panties were moist, and her nipples erect. In other circumstances, feeling turned on like this, she might have decided to masturbate, but it seemed like that would sully the fantasy out of which she had just emerged. Splashing her face, she went back through to the living room, turned the computer on, and googled the phrase "Taxi licenses for sale, Madrid."

Dozens of results came up, both from individual sellers and from companies offering advice on the subject. She called a couple of the numbers to get an idea of the price of a license, which was anywhere between 120,000 and 150,000 euros, depending on the state of the vehicle and the rest day stipulated in the license. She was relieved to learn that, unlike driving a truck, taxi driving did not require a special license. As long as you passed a test on routes through the city and tourist attractions, all you needed was a basic private car license. Aside from that, the relevant laws had to be learned and a number of psychometric tests passed, all of which sounded straightforward enough. It was, in any case, a question of applying oneself, whether enrolling at a taxi school or buying the manuals and studying independently.

She rose feeling excited at the prospect and did a few calculations. She had enough in savings to buy a license without a loan from the bank, and she would still have a little put aside to see her through any unforeseen difficulties. There was also the fact that registering as self-employed meant she could ask for her monthly unemployment payments, to which she was now entitled, in advance. She began pacing the apartment, chewing her fingernails. She could forget about the world of programming, given the situation in the market, but she wanted a change of direction anyway. Not only that; she had just been given the clearest of indications as to which way she ought to go.

Something's going to happen, said her mother inside her head.

Going back to the computer, she went on the

City Council's website and saw that a taxi license examination was being held the following month. That meant thirty days to study for some tests, which, for a person of her abilities, would be relatively straightforward. Without further ado, and on an impulse rather out of keeping with her calculating character, and thinking to save herself the cost of the driving school, which seemed gratuitous, she immediately ordered the manuals.

3

SHE PASSED THE EXAM with ease. The psychometric test (fifty questions to answer in twenty minutes) was a snap. The one on taxi laws (fifteen questions in twenty minutes), she also could have done with her eyes closed. She had a gift for memorizing things, and this was what she did here, memorize each and every one of the articles as she once had entire modules on her programming course, about which she had understood nothing. More challenging were the exercises in which one had to identify places in the city on a map with all the street names blanked out. But she scored six out of six on that, as well. She found the idea of this kind of map extremely suggestive; life itself was a map on which all the street names had been blanked out, everybody filling it in with their own events, events that then turned into the features on the map.

One event that had occurred every morning, while she was studying the taxi laws or practicing psychometric tests, was the music floating in through the bathroom air vent from the third-floor apartment. Always opera. Much of it she recognized from film sound tracks; other pieces were more vaguely familiar, things she had heard here and there without ever paying them any mind. And most of the pieces, since it was her first time hearing them, she found so moving that it was as though they had been part of her musical experience in a past life.

During this time, she bought a number of CDs (*Carmen, La Traviata, Aida, The Barber of Seville*), and, when she listened to them on her stereo, not only did she not find them moving but they put her on edge. In contrast, when the compositions came drifting in through the air vent, she would put aside her exam preparations, go into the bathroom, sit down on the bidet or the toilet, and find herself completely overcome with feelings of love—love for whom, she did not know, but certainly some person from another dimension—as though the real music belonged to a reality different from her own and was filtering in through the very cracks separating these dimensions. This idea, which she had come across in an article online, generated in her a fascination from which she found it impossible to extract herself.

When leaving the building now, she always took the stairs, stopping briefly outside the front door of the third-floor apartment below. The music tended to be on loud, and yet it failed to be annoying. She never bumped into the person who lived in the apartment, and she came to think it must be some university student who put music on to study. In her student days, she had met people who were able to concentrate perfectly well with the radio on.

Two days before the taxi license exam, slightly tired by now of running through the same psychometric tests over and over again and, similarly, of naming streets on the blanked-out maps, she decided to take the plunge and go and introduce herself to the person downstairs, the owner of all the opera music. First she had a shower and put on some perfume, but opted for a tracksuit, the kind one wears around the house, to avoid the impression she had gotten ready especially. Her legs trembled with every step down the stairs, as though instead of being on her way to the third floor, she was going all the way to the basement. She rang the doorbell timidly, to be met with the sound of some complaint by a tenor voice—she had studied the different tessituras by this point—seemingly imploringly, though imploring what, exactly, Lucía didn't know, because the person was speaking in Italian.

Nothing happened, so Lucía rang a second, a third, and even a fourth time, at which point she had given up hope of anybody answering, and in her irritation, she proceeded to hold down the doorbell, while trying to picture what kind of person would put music on full volume and then go out to the store. She was about to give up, when somebody inside turned the volume down and she heard footsteps approach the door.

Before she could recover, the door opened a little way and the head of a bird man appeared in the resultant gap. His expression was neutral, one of neither annoyance nor happiness. When he saw that Lucía wasn't selling anything, he opened the door a little farther, allowing her a full view of his body. Forty or fifty years old, tall and slim, his nose was an eagle's beak and his hair was white and very messy, like he had spent the entire day tousling it. He had on a pair of blue jeans and a black short-sleeved shirt.

"Sorry to bother you," Lucía said, "but I live above you, and my sink's leaked. I wanted to know if it's affected your kitchen, for the insurance."

The bird man let her in, and Lucía went straight through to the open-plan kitchen, which was to the left of the living room.

"The water would be there if it had come through," she said, pointing to the part of the ceiling where her plumbing roughly ran.

The bird man was standing behind her, checking out her pretend-thin ass, Lucía guessed. A suspicion that was confirmed when she turned around and saw him suddenly avert his gaze, looking up to where she was pointing.

"Well," he said, making a show of looking carefully, "I can't see anything."

Meanwhile, the music continued to play, bringing about an emotion in Lucía identical to the one she felt when she heard it from her bathroom.

"What are you listening to?" she asked, pointing to the stereo.

"Puccini, sung by Pavarotti," he said. "*Turandot.*"

"What's he saying now?" she ventured to ask.

"He's saying, 'My secret is hidden within me, / My name no one shall know, / On your mouth I will tell it / When the light shines.'"

Pavarotti went on singing in Italian as the man observed Lucía with his bird gaze.

"What's your name?" she asked, to fill the silence.

He took a step nearer and, bringing his face so close that his lips brushed against hers, said, "Call me Calaf."

She stood stock-still, as though she had died, for a few moments. Then she said, "Well, if any water appears, let me know so that I can get the insurance company to sort it out."

"Fine," he said, not retreating an inch.

Lucía was in shock when she got back to her apartment, and she immediately went through to the bathroom. Sitting down on the toilet, she listened as the music stopped for a moment, before starting again at the point Calaf had translated for her—which she could remember word for word: *My secret is hidden within me, / My name no one shall know, / On your mouth I will tell it / When the light shines.*

Calaf.

Again, the idiot tears. Calaf was a bird's name. At least it was the name of the bird she had been given as a girl.

Puccini. *Turandot.*

Lucía went to her computer and looked up the name of the opera. She read, in a state of some agitation, a summary of the plot, the main characters in which were called Turandot and Calaf. The action takes place in Peking, where Princess Turandot, an avowed man-hater, will only agree to marry the suitor who can answer three riddles set by her. Any wrong answer results in the suitor in question being put to death, and the heads of those who fail the test are placed on spikes around the ceremonial square. Birds fly around overhead, occasionally landing to peck at the heads. At one point, an unknown prince, Calaf, appears, and decides to try his hand. . . .

Calaf, the bird she'd had as a pet, had come from China. How was it possible that in all those years she had never inquired about the reason behind the name, which she had just learned from her neighbor?

Luckily, she was a person whose practical side kicked in anytime she was feeling disconcerted. She remembered her exams were in two days' time, and went back to the blanked-out maps, tests, and taxi laws.

After passing the exam with flying colors, she was furiously busy for two weeks, caught up in the buying of a taxi license from a recently retired driver, for whom this money represented his pension plan. It was a question of weighing up the state of the car, which tended to come hand in hand with the license, the miles on the clock, the rest day stipulated in the license. In the end, she went with a hybrid Toyota, which was in very good condition; it had covered 150,000 miles but still had a good amount of life left in it. As a way of looking after it—it was going to be her sole source of income from now on—she sold her car so that the taxi could be parked in the garage that came with the apartment.

4

SHE TOOK THE TAXI OUT for the first time at 8:45 A.M. on October 1, a chilly day. In time, she would adjust her hours according to what she found out on the job, though in principle her idea was to avoid very early starts.

Within a few minutes of pulling out of the garage, she was hailed on avenida de América by a middle-aged woman who wanted to go to Callao. Nice run, thought Lucía, taking it as a good sign. The woman was wearing a long beige coat with a wide collar she had turned up against the cold, and a wide-brimmed hat of the same color that had a feather poking out of it. The feather, Lucía thought, went well with the woman's birdlike nose, the kind people call "aquiline"—like Lucía's mother's, and indeed like the one Lucía had inherited from her. She toyed with the idea that the woman was a reincarnation of her progenitor, here to welcome her into this new phase in her working life.

Something's going to happen, she heard inside her head, glimpsing the shadow of a swallow flying across the vault of her skull.

The woman in the back gave a sigh of relief.

"I was waiting a full quarter of an hour on that corner," she said, taking the hat off and shaking out her hair. "But the taxis going by were all taken."

The woman clearly felt like talking. At the second set of traffic lights, she said that her period had come that morning, and, at the third, that she worked as a producer for a theater company with offices in the Palacio de la Prensa building. This startled Lucía: She had learned that her neighbor (or ex-neighbor, since he had moved out by now), the bird man who listened to opera in the mornings, was an actor. As a way of covering her discomfort, she asked whether the woman thought she had the looks to be an actress.

"Yes, in principle," conceded the woman. "You've got a lovely, bright face."

When Lucía explained that this light originated in the clash between the carnal and the spiritual, and wasn't unusual in people who were pretend thin, the woman gave her a look that was half amused and half incredulous.

"What did you say?"

"Have you never met a pretend-thin person before?"

"Well, now that you mention it, maybe I have. . . ."

"In any case," said Lucía, "pretend thinness isn't to be confused with hidden obesity. Hidden

obesity is a clinical diagnosis, while pretend thinness is a metaphysical concept."

The woman burst out laughing.

"It's never occurred to me before," she said,
"but show business is full of women who are pretend thin. And all of them are attractive in a way
that straightforwardly thin women aren't. You've
just given me the key to their success."

"Whereas," said Lucía, galvanized by this
response, "you never get pretend-fat people; it's
impossible. A person either is or isn't fat."

She had barely finished speaking these words
when she realized that the woman in the back was
fat. Not very fat, but fat at any rate. She glanced in
the rearview mirror to check if she'd offended her,
and it seemed she hadn't, though silence then fell
between them for a few moments, after which the
woman asked Lucía if she liked opera; *Turandot*
was on the car stereo. Lucía said no, she had it on
because it reminded her of someone.

"Who, if you don't mind me asking?"

"A man."

The woman smiled.

"Just any man?"

"No, a man ... whom I like," Lucía said
falteringly.

"You don't have to tell me everything straight
away," said the woman, "I often use taxis to get
things off my chest. The car is a kind of bubble; it
creates a provisional sort of intimacy between two

strangers. I've told colleagues of yours things that not even my closest girlfriends know about."

Again, this had a galvanizing effect on Lucía, who replied, "Now that you say it, the second I saw you, I thought the two of us could be sisters. We've got the same nose, see? I get mine from my mother."

"Not me. I get mine from my father, and I've more than once thought about having it operated on."

"What are you saying? Aquiline noses are magnificent."

As they exchanged smiles in the rearview mirror, Lucía felt a burst of joy at the realization that, unlike other places in which she had worked, here it was possible to talk with complete freedom. Nonetheless, she contained the urge to make reference to her former neighbor, the man who had introduced himself as Calaf but who, according to her inquiries, was in fact called Braulio. Instead, she said, "Know what?"

"What?"

"You're my first fare."

"Your first of the day?"

"No, my first ever. Today's my first day as a taxi driver. When I picked you up, seeing your nose and the feather in your hat, I toyed with the idea of your being a reincarnation of my mother. My mother was a bird woman."

"A bird woman?"

"Yes."

"Okay . . . And what's that?"

"Well, I've started, I suppose. . . . Then again, I've never told anyone about this."

"But we've already established that it's normal to divulge secrets in a taxi."

"Yes, I was thinking that; I just couldn't be totally sure."

"Well, you hit the nail on the head. Nobody's ever told me I look like the reincarnation of anyone. So, your mother was a bird woman. . . ."

Lucía then told her the story of her tenth birthday, feeling quite moved as she recounted in detail the moment when she saw her mother lift up her skirt and lower her panties and how a blackbird had immediately appeared in the sky, plummeting like a meteorite straight into her mother's head.

"Jeez!" said the woman when Lucía finished. "That's quite the imagination you've got there! This is a ploy to stop me from getting out, right? Doubtless there's plenty more where that came from."

"It happened exactly like I said," said Lucía, worried she had let herself get carried away.

"And the thing about the soap bubble full of smoke appearing out of the bird's beak?"

"Well," she conceded, "I admit I might have imagined that part. I don't know, I was only ten, but believe me when I say that in my memory, that's what really happened."

"Children get reality and fantasy mixed up."

Lucía fell quiet then, suddenly feeling very low. Would the woman go away thinking she had just met a crazy person? Had Lucía gone way overboard?

The woman must have picked up on this drop in her spirits, and changed the subject, her previous confidence returning.

"Anyway, you were telling me that *Turandot* reminded you of a man you had a thing for."

"Ah, yes. But I think I've put on enough of a show for today."

"Hey, don't be like that. Today's the first day of your new job, a very special day. I'd like you to have good memories of your first-ever customer. Plus, when it comes down to it, who's to say I'm not your mother reincarnated?"

"How amazing would that be."

"All the more reason for you to spill the beans on this guy."

Lucía, her openness returning, told the woman about the encounter with Calaf (Braulio) in his apartment, with her making up the excuse of the leak.

"He told me his name was Calaf, like the character in *Turandot,* but I found out later on that his real name was Braulio. He brushed his lips against mine at the same time as he said 'Calaf,' and while 'Nessun dorma' was playing in the background—one of the most beautiful arias in *Turandot*. Then he disappeared from my life."

"Just like that?" said the woman.

"Pretty much," said Lucía. "A few days afterward, I stopped hearing the music from the apartment below. At first, I put it down to its being the weekend—it was a Saturday. Maybe, I said to myself, this Calaf spent his weekends away. But then Monday came, Black Monday, as I've thought of it since, and still no music. On the Tuesday, I went downstairs and knocked, but nobody answered. I asked the super, and he told me the man's name was Braulio Botas, and that he'd moved out. I found it surprising that somebody should be called Botas, especially with a first name like Braulio, but then straightaway Botas appealed to me, as well. Braulio Botas. I couldn't stop saying it to myself."

"Braulio Botas?"

"Yes."

"The theater actor?"

"So it says on his Facebook page, but he can't be very famous, because I'd never heard of him before. Or seen him on TV. So when you said you worked in theater, my heart skipped a beat. Did you notice?"

"Well, now that you mention it . . ."

"And do you know him?"

"Not personally. He works in alternative theater; the kind of shows we do are more commercial. But I think he's good, and so do the people I work with. Our view is that he could make the jump, given the right role. Doubtless his agent isn't up to much."

"I'd never heard of him before."

"That isn't so surprising. Theater's quite like that, a bit of a closed circuit, its own ecosystem. Someone can be well known or relatively well known within the sector and a complete unknown outside of it. Especially if the person isn't on TV."

"And is Braulio Botas well known?"

"Well, he hasn't had any big successes, though that might be through a lack of opportunity."

Lucía turned pensive.

"You won't tell anyone about this, will you?"

"As I say, I don't know him personally."

"But if you did happen to meet him . . ."

"You're jumping the gun. Don't worry, your secret's safe with me."

"Also, why is it that Braulio Botas rolls off the tongue like it does? I just can't stop saying it, Braulio Botas."

"Because of the two *B*'s," said the woman. "Plus, if you look closely, the first vowel in Braulio is an *a,* and the last one's an *o,* while the first one in Botas is an *o* and the last one an *a.* It's a pretty impressive interplay of sounds."

"How do you know so much?" asked Lucía, her admiration sincere.

"Oh, in the theater we look at these things a lot—when we're coming up with names for characters.

But tell me: If you liked Braulio Botas so much, why didn't you kiss him back?"

"Well, I'm a taxi driver now, but I used to be a programmer. And certain decisions I take are based on algorithms created specifically for the task. I could have kissed him back, of course I could have, and maybe that was what he expected. But it seemed to me that, if things unfolded in the normal way, I, flustered as I was, needed to turn him down, so that he would come up to my apartment later that day, or the next, using any excuse, even just to apologize for having been so forward."

"I know nothing about algorithms," said the woman, "but your attitude, I'm sorry, it seems a bit old-fashioned."

"Old-fashioned isn't always bad. Take Burgos Cathedral."

A somewhat fraught silence ensued, broken by the woman, who asked if there was any relationship between algorithms and everyday life.

"Of course there is!" said Lucía. "Give me an example of a problem you deal with every day."

"I'm always late for work. That's why I blow so much on taxis."

"Okay, so that's the input data: You're always late for work. Now, have you got an alarm clock on your bedside table?"

"Yes."

"And does it work?"

"Yes."

"And you set it every night before you go to bed?"

"Of course."

"Do you set it to give yourself enough time to do everything you need to do before leaving the house?"

"Yes."

"But do you actually leave on time?"

"No, in the end there's always something I get caught up in."

"So, as you see," said Lucía, "all these questions, if we had a piece of paper and a pen, could go in a descending column, which programmers and systems analysts call a 'flowchart.'"

"A flowchart?" repeated the woman, laughing raucously.

"What?" said Lucía once the woman had calmed down a little.

"I'm sorry, it just made me think about vaginal flow. Charts of vaginal flows."

Lucía did not find this funny, or perhaps she did—she wasn't sure—but she gave a pretend guffaw. She didn't find it difficult to pretend. They laughed all the way along Serrano. Once the laughter had subsided, the woman asked her to go on with the algorithm.

"And is it only work you're late for, or everything?"

"Everything, in truth."

"Then you need a psychologist to work out

what's going on with you. And that's the output data, the solution, we would say."

"And that's an algorithm?" asked the woman.

"That's an algorithm."

Again the woman started laughing, assuring Lucía that she already knew she needed to see a psychologist.

"And not necessarily a male psychologist," Lucía added. "It's up to us to stop this from being a man's world."

"You're so funny," said the woman, moving to the informal *tú* address for the first time. They were on Callao now, and Lucía pulled up opposite the Palacio de la Prensa. "I'm Roberta, by the way. What's your name?"

"Lucía."

"Well, give me your card, Lucía. I use taxis all the time. I'll call you."

Lucía gave her a card and was on the verge of letting the woman have the ride for free, but her practical side won out. She was doing this to earn a living, she reminded herself. The woman paid with a credit card, which gave Lucía a chance to try out the card reader.

"Good luck!" called the woman as she bustled out onto the sidewalk, late for work.

WHAT WOULD BE LUCKY, thought Lucía, would be to see Braulio Botas again and to succeed in stealing a little of his time, in spite of the cultural chasm that surely lies between us.

Braulio. Braulio Botas.

Those two words, mere sounds though they were, had already become part of her vital organs, of her viscera, and they performed a function in the same way the liver or the pancreas performed certain functions. If they were stripped from inside her, she would die. In bed, as she was falling asleep and in the instants after she awoke, she recalled their meeting with such violence that the fantasy took on all the qualities of real life. And opera had been the start of it all! Opera, a genre that had always made her feel nothing but angst, until the day she heard Maria Callas's voice coming in through the bathroom vent.

From the first minute of taking the wheel in her taxi, the single fantasy she entertained was that of picking up Braulio Botas. She would keep the vehicle spick-and-span, solely with this possibility in mind. She would turn it into Madrid's cleanest taxi, the most agreeable, the sweetest-smelling. And, of course, *Turandot* would always be playing, so that the actor, when she did finally pick him up, would feel at home.

The situations in which she and Braulio met, in her fantasy, varied in the extreme. If it was raining, she imagined him on the sidewalk, umbrella in hand, trying to hail passing taxis, all of which just so happened to be taken, apart from hers. She showed up just in time to save him from a real drenching.

She thought how good it would be if she called herself Turandot, like the daughter of the Chinese emperor, so that if it came to his asking her name, she would say, "Turandot, my name's Turandot."

When he showed surprise, she would explain that her father, as a great admirer of Puccini, had chosen it.

"In reality," she would add, "it's Lucía Turandot. People call me Lucía, obviously."

The rest of her first day was uneventful. She made less money than she had expected, which she put down to lack of experience, since she didn't yet know the best times and places to be guaranteed a good number of fares. She followed the occasional veteran driver to see how he went about things, but she found that most of the drivers tended to kill time in the designated taxi stands, an example she had no intention of following, in part because she liked to stay on the move and in part because people tended to socialize in the taxi stands, which, for now, held no interest for her.

Come the evening, when she was back at home, her cell phone rang, and it turned out to be Roberta, her first fare. She asked how Lucía's day had gone, adding that she had enjoyed meeting her and would give all her friends Lucía's number, in case they ever needed a taxi. Lucía, surprised by this success, indulged the fantasy of having so many regular customers that she would have no need to hustle.

"Hustle in the sense of going hunting for fares, as opposed to them requesting my services," she said out loud, just so it was clear.

5

SHE ALWAYS DRESSED SMARTLY, sometimes ensuring that the right side of her face
was visible to the passenger in the back, along with
the long, silver tear-shaped earring she wore on
that side. She would fasten her hair, which was a
coppery chestnut brown, in a ponytail on the other
side, using a large hair clip, also silver, to match
the earring. The overall effect, the asymmetry of
it, was tremendous.

At other times, she gathered her hair into a
ballerina's bun on the crown of her head, scrap-
ing it tightly upward so that the nape of her neck
was uncovered. The sight of her bare neck, in the
confines of the taxi, could, she supposed, be pro-
foundly exciting for someone, even without any
tattoos there. The thought of the tattoo was related
to the memory of a fellow student at her high
school, a girl who'd had a highly realistic vagina
tattooed in that most mysterious part of the neck.
The girl usually concealed it by having her hair
down, but sometimes, seemingly getting a kick out
of it, she would put it up, sending the boys in the

desks behind her into a frenzy. It was a picture of her own vagina, copied by the tattoo artist from a photograph she herself had taken.

Lucía was sometimes unsure which of the two hairstyles Braulio Botas would find more seductive, and she therefore alternated between them, leaving it up to fate which of the two he would be confronted with the day he got into her taxi. Because he would be getting into her taxi. There was simply no question about it.

As for her eyes, and given that *Turandot* took place in Peking and the main character was a Chinese princess, she started doing her makeup to look like one. Her cheeks, dusted with a mixture of rice and oat powder she had made following an online video tutorial, gave her the stark white pallor typical of certain characters in Chinese theater.

As she drove the streets of Madrid, she said to herself, over and over, Something's going to happen. What was going to happen was that he would appear on one street corner or another with his hand raised. She had joined the books of a taxi company purely on the chance that a call might come over the radio one day to pick up a certain Braulio Botas, at X building, on Y square. (She had decided that he lived on a square). And she would be the nearest taxi to that address, would field the call, drive there, and, speaking into the building's intercom, would say, "Braulio Botas?"

"Yes," he would reply.

"Your taxi is here," she would say.

And he would come and get in the taxi, and she would have everything set up so that when he arrived, "Nessun dorma" would be playing, just the same as when Lucía had asked him his name in his apartment and he, his lips brushing hers, had whispered it to her.

Calaf.

On occasion, due to pure emotional exhaustion, she would turn the stereo off. But then she would begin reciting the lyrics, a translation of which she had found on the Internet:

Let no one sleep,

Let no one sleep!

Even you, oh Princess,

In your cold room,

Watch the stars,

That tremble with love

And with hope.

But my secret is hidden within me,

My name no one shall know,

No . . . no . . .

On your mouth I will tell it

When the light shines.

And my kiss shall dissolve the silence that
      makes you mine!

Vanish, oh night!

Set, stars! Set, stars!

At dawn, I will win!

I will win!

I will win!

She was able to recite it in Italian or in Spanish—
it didn't matter which—just as she could wear
her hair in one style or another depending on her
mood.

And her mood was good, given that, although
her inner mantra was not making anything happen, she was quite certain that it was only a matter
of time. This sensation grew more acute throughout
that cold and rainy autumn, when the buildings,
viewed through the water sheeting her windshield,
changed shape entirely, as though made of a kind
of plastic, giving a dreamlike quality to everything
around her. She turned on the windshield wipers
only when the view became so blurred that she
could no longer drive safely. She imagined Braulio
Botas on every single corner she passed, wearing
a trench coat that was slightly too big on him, as
trench coats always were on slim people, and holding an umbrella in his left hand, while with his

right he tried to hail the first taxi that passed, a taxi that would be none other than hers.

Nor was it true to say that nothing ever happened. One day, after eating lunch in a bar at Atocha station, and in spite of her preference for staying on the move, she pulled up at the taxi stand outside the Palace Hotel and picked up a man waiting there with an overnight bag. He was very well dressed, with a tailored coat on top of what appeared to be an expensive suit. He had a nice face, and in profile a birdlike aspect that reminded her of Braulio Botas. No sooner had he gotten in than she heard her mother's voice inside her head: *Something's going to happen.*

"Terminal four, please," said the man, shutting the door behind him. "The Air Bridge."

"Good afternoon," she replied, her tone, without quite being rude, clearly pointing out that he had skipped the greeting.

"Sorry. Good afternoon," the man said. His voice was infinitely sad.

Lucía pulled the taxi out without another word, turning up the volume on the stereo a little.

"*Turandot,*" the man immediately said.

"*Turandot,* yes," confirmed Lucía.

"Did you know that Puccini died without finishing it?"

"I did. I read about it."

"And did you know that it was, nonetheless, his

life's work, that everything he'd done previously seemed poor to him in comparison?"

"So I've also read."

Then, for no apparent reason, the man buried his face in his hands and began to sob. Lucía went on driving without saying anything, though she turned the volume down on the stereo—out of respect.

"Sorry," stammered the man once he had managed to compose himself.

"No problem," she said. "Certain passages in this opera make me emotional, too."

"It isn't that; it's that I'm going home with very bad news."

"Get it off your chest if you like. We'll probably never meet again."

The man then told her that he lived in Barcelona, although he often traveled to Madrid on business.

"Last week," he said, "making the most of the fact I was here, I went to a doctor, because I haven't been feeling well for a while. I thought I'd do it here in Madrid, so as not to worry my family; I had a feeling it was something bad. I just got the results earlier on, and I've got a tumor."

"Is it malignant?" asked Lucía automatically.

"Yes, malignant."

Having said this, the man broke down and started crying even more desperately than before. Lucía didn't know whether to ask where the tumor

was or if he'd been given a specific amount of time
to live. She didn't know how to act, so she opted
to stay quiet. By this time, they were at the Puerta
de Alcalá. She would normally have continued
along O'Donnell and gotten onto the M-30, but
that would have meant passing the city morgue,
which she thought wouldn't be appropriate at that
moment. She turned onto Velázquez instead.

"*Turandot*," said the man, "an unfinished work.
It made me think of an unfinished life."

Such sensitivity left Lucía speechless. Finally,
she said there was no such thing as an unfinished
life.

"My mother," she went on, "died young, when
I was ten. You get lives that are longer or shorter
than others, but as for unfinished . . ."

The man's sobs then became so intense that
she had to pass him a box of tissues, since his had
run out.

Lucía looked at the clock. It was 5:30 P.M. and
she had made barely ninety euros all day, even
though she had started at 8:00 A.M. But when she
got to calle de Colón, she turned the car around
and headed back in the direction of the hotel.

"What are you doing?" asked the man.

"We're going back to the hotel," she said firmly.
"You can't go home in this state."

The man looked at her in the rearview mirror,
and Lucía had the impression that he was seeing
her for the first time. Following his gaze, it came

to her that it had slid down from the visible side of her face to her nape, and from there to the base of her neck. (She was wearing her hair up that day.) Her senses, like the seismographs in museums that register tremors deep in the bowels of the earth, told her that something was moving deep in the man's spirit, and perhaps in the depths of his flesh, as well. She felt hesitant, and fearful, too, but she let the unexpected situation unfold in silence. Pulling up opposite the hotel, next to the pedestrian crossing, she gave the man her card.

"Send me a message with your room number," she said, addressing him with the informal *tú*. "And wait for me there. I'll park and then come up."

"And if there aren't any free rooms?" the man asked.

"Wait for me out front. We'll find someplace else, don't worry."

The man got out with his overnight bag and crossed the street, past the front of the car, without daring to look at her. Lucía observed him carefully and decided he was a refined man, with the refinement that came with being cultured. The word *cultured* in her inner monologue was followed by an image in her mind of a flamingo, then that of a stork, and then the image of a history teacher.

One of the history teachers at her high school had always worn a suit that was too big for him, though he moved around in it with the pliancy and lightness of a happy thought moving within the walls of one's skull. There had been something of the bird man about him, as well, like Braulio, like this man with terminal cancer. Lucía had always been captivated by the way he moved back and forth across the small raised platform at the front of the classroom, in the same way seagulls moved about the beach at the end of the afternoon, after all the beachgoers had gone home.

She turned off the meter, drove along to the Congreso parking lot, and had to go four floors underground—not far short of hell, she thought—because all the spaces were taken. Not a bad business, she thought. Naturally, she kept an eye on her cell phone, though no messages came through; she then realized there was no coverage so far below street level. Nonetheless, it was possible that the man had been overcome by fright and, getting to the hotel entrance, turned around and found another taxi to take him to the airport.

Well, it was his decision. She, too, was a little frightened, though not overly, because in her mind's eye she was seeing a very beautiful flamingo, completely white except for its wing tips, which were orangish, the orange of a cheerful piece of stationery, and a splash of that same bright color on the crown of its head, the same place her bun was positioned.

The curious part was that she did not picture the flamingo as being in the water, but up on the dais her old history teacher used to move about on with the jerky unsteadiness of elegant birds. In any case, it was a vision that produced a strangely peaceful sensation in her spirit. She was doing the right thing, acting with an organic sensitivity toward a fellow being who was unwell.

She climbed the stairs back to street level, since the elevator took an age to arrive, and bought a packet of condoms at a vending machine she came across before reaching the exit. Fifteen seconds after she walked out onto the street, she heard a message come through on her cell.

Room 101.

One, zero, one. As though the cancer sufferer's world belonged to the system of binary code, in which she happened to be an expert. What luck. Everything was as it should be.

6

She was wearing a very expensive suede jacket that day, which kept her warm without ever overheating her. It was a luxury she had allowed herself for beginning this new phase with the taxi. Under the jacket, which was a cinnamon red, she had on a very thin black cashmere sweater, which clung to her breasts and hips. As she moved about, the cashmere and the fabric of her bra were in a kind of dialogue that kept her nipples awake. The outfit was rounded off by a pair of light semi-elastic jeans, which, without being overly tight, just gripped her magnificent pretend-thin thighs.

She always dressed smartly, counting on the possibility that today would be the day she encountered Braulio, Braulio Botas, and this was the same reason she had chosen quite a special ensemble of matching underwear, pumpkin orange and gauzy as a layer of skin. She wore a pair of very cheerful sneakers to drive in, the patterns on them slightly childish, conferring a mischievous aspect on her rather small feet. But she kept a pair of low-heeled pumps in the trunk that matched her suede jacket;

though they looked smart, she could walk comfortably in them. She had changed into these in the parking lot. She had also put on a silk scarf that she kept in the glove compartment, out of which she also took a small purse containing, as well as two small perfume sprays (one of them for her nether regions), some essentials should she ever need to touch up her makeup.

She liked the Palace Hotel; she had been there four or five times for meetings related to her former job, though she had seen only a couple of the function rooms inside, plus the domed salon farthest back off the street, which to her mind was the height of elegance. She would have had no problem living out her days beneath that fabulous vault, so evocative of an enormous birdcage, sleeping on any one of the sofas distributed around the space, waking and stretching out her limbs on them, eating breakfast and lunch and supper eternally in that ambience, like someone eating breakfast and lunch and supper and sleeping and waking in her mother's uterus.

Her mother.

Since she knew where the bathroom was, she first went there to pee, give her private parts a good clean (she carried alcohol-free wet wipes with her), and sort out her makeup. When she looked in the mirror, she found the person before her attractive, very much so, very attractive and very slim, and there was a set to her mouth that it assumed independently at times, with no conscious input from her (at moments when there was a sense that something was going to happen), an expression not quite apprehensive and not quite calm. It was a very demanding mouth that at the same time offered itself up wholly and unreservedly.

When she left the bathroom, she felt so utterly in control of the situation that she decided to stop by the domed salon on her way to the elevator that would take her to room 101. There, too, she found calm and apprehension mingling in the air. There was a mix of hotel guests, identifiable by their more informal attire, and businesspeople, the latter meeting to close deals or discuss new ventures. Everyone was chatting in a relaxed way, intermittently lifting a cup of tea or coffee to their lips, either that or an early-evening cocktail.

She did not go so far as to say that something was going to happen, because it was already happening. What she couldn't have imagined was that within what was happening, something else might occur. And what occurred was that among those people lounging in the designer chairs and elegant sofas, under the windows of that luxurious hotel, Braulio Botas, her actor, suddenly materialized. Lucía could not have said whether her heart stopped before discovering him, because she had already intuited his presence, or after. She knew that there had been two movements, one of prescience and another of conscious perception, although it was a mystery to her whether one had happened after the other or both at the same time.

Her heart stopped for a few instants but then started once more, as when a computer inexplicably shuts down and all the experts can put it down to is random error. It could be said that for a few tenths of a second, Lucía died, and that when she came back to life, Braulio Botas was still there, chatting away with another man, perhaps another actor, who was smiling at him while moving some documents about on the table. Braulio's suit jacket was navy blue or black, very dark, in any case, and he had a white shirt on with a slightly high collar and no tie. A classic, elegant combination, Lucía said to herself. She could not see his pants or shoes with the table in the way.

What to do? Upstairs, in room 101, she had the cancer sufferer waiting for her, but right there in front of her, just a few meters away, in all his glory, she had Braulio Botas. She noticed that his jacket was slightly baggy on him, and this prompted an infinite tenderness for him, which, in turn, made her vagina suddenly extraordinarily wet. She could feel this wetness seeping through the fabric of her panties and onto her elasticated jeans. In that moment, she would quite happily have stridden across the short distance separating them, dragged him up to room 101, thrown the cancer sufferer out of the window, and eaten the actor alive.

She thought about literally eating him. She

would have thrown him onto the bed and begun
with his cock, which she imagined erect. Why the
cock? In order to eliminate all genital euphoria, so
that they could be calm for the remainder of the
feast, fully conscious of all they were doing. In
fact, after ingesting his cock, she would go and sit
astride his face to give him a full view of her vulva,
perfectly shaved, though without any tattoos on it
yet; she was planning to have the words

Nessun

dorma

tattooed on her mons veneris, just like this, one
word above the other, as a surprise for Braulio
Botas the day they ended up in bed together. Inev-
itably, what with one thing and another, she had
kept putting it off.

But she digressed. After she had taken down
his cock, she thought, she would, indeed, go and
straddle his face, perching on the pillows she
would previously have positioned under his head,
so that he, with the manners of a true gastronome,
could sample first her vulva, then move in a layer,
lingering over all the different flavors, savoring
them, before coming to the clitoris, swollen by now
and offered up by her, forefinger and thumb, like
someone extracting the best part of a fruit to present to her lover.

"All yours," she would say, her fingers slick from her inner juices.

Then, each of them unencumbered by those desirous, so incredibly delicious genital parts, their souls would be ready to tackle the rest of their bodies with all the serenity of sophisticates. She would then offer him her tongue to chew on (words would, in any case, have failed by now), and he would offer her his. She would offer him her nipples, and he would offer her his. She, the flesh around her sternum, the most delicious of all, and he, the same. They would then tear salty strips (salty from the sweat) from each other's backs, moving down to each other's ribs, which, because they wouldn't be able to lick them, given their mutual eating of each other's tongues already, they would simply, and tenderly, kiss. This as a prelude to the ingestion of each other's lips.

The tenderness was prompted by the realization, which had just come to her, that Braulio Botas had never had anyone to take care of him. She read it in his face, in the way he held himself, in his every gesture. Here was a man who had always been alone; perhaps his mother had died in childbirth, or, as with Lucía's mother, when he was young. Whether from birth or later on, it didn't matter; he was an orphan. But this would be her way of caring for him, eating him whole while letting him eat her, until the moment came when, having eaten so much of each other—given that, if

the nutritionists were right, we are what we eat—
she would have turned into him and he into her.
Then, after a short rest, they would start eating
each other all over again.

The cannibal delirium that filled her thoughts
for a few brief moments as, hypnotized, she contemplated the actor might have been due to a
television documentary on the conquistadors in
Mexico that she had seen a couple of nights earlier. Most surprising to the arriving Spanish, it
had said, were the indigenous practices of cannibalism and sodomy. For some reason, those
two words, *cannibalism* and *sodomy,* kept being
repeated in tandem throughout the documentary,
one always followed by the other, meaning that,
remembering the program now, while observing
Braulio Botas (who had not seen her), she imagined being entered anally by the cock she had
eaten just seconds before, and at this her wetness
began to overflow, bursting the banks of her panties and escaping down her inner thighs.

Amid this emotional turbulence, the aria from
Turandot kept playing over and over in her head,
as though there was a stereo actually inside her
and it was on at full blast:

Nessun dorma!

Nessun dorma!

Tu pure, oh principessa

Nella tua freda stanza

Guardi le stelle che tremano

D'amore e di speranza!

Now, in a matter of seconds, tenths of a single second perhaps, different ways of approaching the actor spun through her mind, but they all seemed indiscreet to her, not to say ridiculous, so that she discounted each in turn; after all, she hadn't entirely lost her mind. And yet she stayed exactly where she was, rooted, waiting for a miracle to come. And this was followed by Braulio, Braulio, Braulio Botas leaning forward, picking up his cocktail (a gin and tonic, or possibly a vodka and tonic), and, before raising it to his mouth, looking around, as though a pair of invisible antennae had made him aware of Lucía's presence. Their eyes met, a fleeting, eternal moment, before that bird face of his turned back to the other man, making no sign of having recognized her.

Staying put any longer was not a good idea, so, seized by a furious kind of arousal, she turned and headed for the elevators. As she got into one, a couple were coming out, an older man and a younger woman in a suede jacket much like her own. When they had stepped out, the woman turned her head and gave Lucía a meaningful stare.

"Mistake me for someone, bitch?" said Lucía, spittle from her mouth hitting the woman's face.

The man and woman, utterly taken aback, failed to formulate any comeback before the doors shut and the elevator began to ascend. Lucía then looked at herself in the mirror and, since she had to say something, although she didn't know what, came out with what she usually came out with when confronted with this image of herself in a mirror: "That fat woman is me."

This time, she said it aggressively.

7

WHEN SHE KNOCKED on the door of room 101, the cancer sufferer was on the phone and took a few moments to come to the door. He begged Lucía's pardon; he had called his wife to tell her he was spending an extra night in Madrid. This, Lucía thought, was really a way of asking her whether they were going to spend the night together.

Rather than answering, she, in turn, asked whether his wife had suspected anything.

"It happens quite often with my work," he said.

Lucía then pushed him back onto the bed and started to undress him like a baby, commanding him not to do anything, to be passive, like a child. He was half frightened, half excited, a state that, in Lucía's experience, drove men and women alike to a kind of agitated imperturbability. While doing nothing outwardly to excite him, in an intimate way she fueled that furious desire, removing each article of clothing with a calculated slowness, even folding and hanging them over the back of an armchair rather than tossing them on the floor like in the movies.

"Leave it all to me, little one," she whispered every time he—more because he thought it was the correct thing to do than out of an overwhelming passion—tried to take the initiative.

And the man lay back once more, at no moment taking his eyes off Lucía's Chinese princess face; she had done her makeup to look like Princess Turandot in a staging of the opera she'd seen on YouTube. Once he was completely naked, she ordered him to sit up a little so they could pull back the bedcovers; she didn't think they should do it on top of them. She then invited him to get under the sheets, though this left his top half uncovered, including the enormous erection, of which he was perhaps more victim than beneficiary. His slim frame was reminiscent of a sparrow that didn't have any feathers, a body she imagined as being similar to Braulio's, or a history teacher's, or perhaps that of an actor doing alternative theater. Lucía looked him in the eyes and imagined she was standing before Braulio Botas, the vulnerable Braulio Botas she had discovered underneath that oversize jacket.

"Now, little one," she said tenderly, "watch closely what Mama Bird's going to do with you."

And Mama Bird proceeded to take off her suede jacket, leaving it folded on the armchair. And, as if it were a black pelt, she peeled off the cashmere sweater, laying this carefully on top of the jacket before kicking off her shoes and taking off her pants, so that she was now down to panties and bra. The cancer sufferer then reached for his genitalia with his right hand, perhaps to brace his erection, but Mama Bird shook her head.

"It's nasty to touch yourself there," she said. "Did no one ever teach you?"

The cancer sufferer took his hand away and watched as she turned around, presenting him with the sight of her undoing her bra, something men so enjoy, because of the slightly humiliating position it forces women into, arms twisted back and around like that, a movement that appears to be one of submission and in a certain sense is. What kind of person would invent such a garment?

When Mama Bird was completely naked, she felt that those atrophied extremities known as shoulder blades were extending out into a pair of invisible wings, which, under the watchful, long-ing gaze of the cancer sufferer, she had only to beat lightly to glide from one end of the room to the other. Ostensibly, this was in order to go and close the curtains a little, but the real objective was to allow the little baby a complete vision of a bird woman's body, of the pretend-thin body in all its splendor, a fairly rare combination, at least of the caliber of Lucía, with her small but indisputable breasts with their aggressive, faintly obscene nip-ples, and her buttocks, which, though large, were nonetheless not nearly large enough, which also went for her thighs, the place where, if one knew how to look, the secret of the pretend-thin person lay.

Picking up her panties, soaking by now, she leaned over the cancer sufferer and held them out for him to smell.

"So," she whispered, bringing her lips close up to his, "never cheated on your wife with a Mama Bird before?"

"Never," he moaned.

"Never been with any Mama Bird on any of your trips?" she insisted.

"Never," he moaned once more, sticking out his tongue to lick the panties.

Lucía felt a cold current on her bare back, just between the invisible wings, and her excitement was suddenly extinguished. Where had the cold come from? From elsewhere. She had felt it before in moments when her mother, from wherever she now was, had exhaled her cold, dead breath in order to alert her to some danger. Who, after all, was this man whose cock, condoms totally forgotten, she had been on the point of allowing to enter her?

The condoms.

She had left them in one or another of her pockets; she couldn't remember which and it wasn't the moment to start rummaging around for them.

She lay down next to the cancer sufferer and asked him if he was good.

"Are you good?"

"In bed?"

"Not in bed. In life."

The man hesitated.

"I don't know," he said. "I think I'm a good father and husband. I worry a lot about the people close to me. But I don't know if that makes me good. Whereas you, Lucía, you're like an angel."

She found it strange that he should address her by her name, but she then remembered the business card she'd given him.

Lucía rested his head on her shoulder—a protective gesture usually employed by men on women—and pulled him close with her right arm, while with her left she reached down to his testicles, which were hard as rocks. She began to caress him there, hearing him moan as he huddled against her, and when Lucía saw that he couldn't take any more, she took his cock in her hand and, with a couple of swift strokes, emptied him out. Emptied him out completely—emptied him of himself and of his fear of the cancer.

"What about you?" he asked.

"Me," she said, "I just enjoyed giving you that. I don't need anything else. Today's your day. Relax."

"You're a miracle," he murmured.

"Miracles do happen."

In a short while, all his former tensions gone,

the man fell asleep on her shoulder. It was starting to get dark outside. Trying not to wake him, Lucía pulled the sheets up over their bodies. Her hands were covered in semen, cold by now, so she turned the man onto his side and put an arm around his slight frame, laying the cold hand between her thighs. She then shut her eyes, thought about her life a little, and, without going to sleep, began drifting off into a daydream of an embrace with Braulio Botas, against whom she rubbed herself until she came—not hard, but with an orgasm that did reach out into the farthest corners of her body.

8

SHE SPENT THE NIGHT with the cancer sufferer; they had breakfast together and afterward she took him to the airport—practically
without either of them saying a word the entire
time. Lucía forbade him from speaking so that he
wouldn't be afraid of her; she knew that married
men could not conceive of a fling they would not
have to pay for in some way or another. They had
no complaints while it was going on, of course,
but then paranoia set in: She's going to blackmail
me. She'll call my wife. I'll have gotten her preg-
nant. Will the in-laws find out? All those movies
with men destroying their lives because of a single momentary loss of control—they had a lot to
answer for.

"Don't worry about it," she said at breakfast
when he started trying to explain. "I don't know
who you are or what your name is, I've never seen
you before, and this didn't happen."

"But . . ."

"Don't say a word; I don't want to know

anything about you. And you shouldn't know any-thing about me. Give me back my business card."

"I don't know what I did with it."

"Well, when you find it, tear it up."

Lucía knew her number would have been saved on his cell phone, as would his on hers, but she was only trying to assuage the likely feelings of guilt with which the man had awakened.

During the drive to the airport, she put "Nessun dorma" on, and as Pavarotti was coming to the end of the aria, she twisted around in her seat and sang along with the tenor: "All'alba vincerò! Vincerò! Vincerò!"

"Now, the three of us together," she said, replaying the aria.

She, the cancer sufferer, and Pavarotti sang the final verses together, and Lucía, on glancing at the man in the rearview mirror, saw that in that moment he was convinced that he would overcome the illness.

When she pulled up at Madrid-Barajas, outside the Air Bridge to Terminal 4, the man asked again if there was anything he could do for her.

"You don't owe me anything," said Lucía.

He, however, could not help but offer to pay for the taxi ride. Lucía, who had not even turned on the meter, gave him a sad smile.

"Have a little shame," she said. "Go on, go and catch your flight."

He got out of the taxi with his hand luggage

and walked toward the terminal like a child whose mother had just dropped him at the school gates. Once he was out of sight, Lucía took out her cell phone, found the text message he had sent with the room number, and saved him as a contact. Never having found out his name, she saved him as "Cancer Sufferer."

She then drove home to wash and change. In the bathroom, applying her makeup, she remembered the days when she would hear *Turandot* coming in through the air vent. Now she was listening to nothing. Nothing. As though the building were empty. Dead. She would happily have stayed there, cradled by that silence, that kind of nothing, that parenthesis in reality. But she had hardly done any hours the previous day, and to make a decent salary as a taxi driver, you had to be disciplined, had to stick to it.

She had not been out long when she picked up a blind man on María de Molina, whom an elderly woman had helped to hail the taxi. Once he was comfortably seated in the back, and after giving Lucía the address he wanted to go to, he began enumerating the difficulties for a blind person in a city like Madrid. He was handsome, somewhere in the region of fifty or fifty-five, and had lost his sight at the age of seven, meaning he still had some memory of the colors and shapes of things. Lucía asked him what he would choose to look at if he had the chance to regain his sight for a short while.

"How long is a short while?" he asked.

"I don't know," she said. "The time this journey takes?"

"In that case, I would look at whatever people are carrying or holding in their hands." This he said with a certain nostalgia.

"You needn't worry about that; I can just tell you."

They were at a red light, and at that moment a girl was walking by, eating a banana. Lucía told the blind man this, and he started to laugh.

"A banana?"

"A banana, yes."

"And she's eating it, you say?"

"Sure."

Again, the blind man laughed.

For the rest of the journey, Lucía called out to him the things she saw people carrying. Some of these she invented, trying to make the world seem more attractive than it really was. She invented, among other things, a goldfish bowl with a red fish swimming around inside it, a tree-shaped coat stand, and a bidet. By the end, she suspected that the blind man had worked out her game, but if so, he offered no reproach. On the contrary, he said what a wonderful woman she was. Lucía helped him out of the taxi and gave him a card, saying he should call anytime he needed to get somewhere. She had handed out dozens of cards to passengers she had gotten on with, but she supposed that people only accepted them out of politeness, and that they would simply put them in their pockets and forget about them—a kind of amnesiac space from which the cards would rarely emerge.

This, however, was not the case with Roberta, who called for the occasional ride to her office in Callao, or for something else the theater company needed. Roberta was forever asking her questions, getting her to tell her about her childhood, her mother, the Peking of *Turandot,* birds, and life in general, as well as where she was just then in her feelings for Braulio Botas. Lucía, with her birdlike gifts, could tell there was something unusual about this relationship, but the part of her that simply found it gratifying prevailed, such that she began to make things up for Roberta that had happened only in her imagination.

In my imagination? Lucía asked herself—being someone who lived the things she was telling people, and told people things with such passion that it removed any hint of a boundary between the real and the imaginary.

"I was there when my mother died," she said one day. "It was a year after the day that bird flew into her head. You remember that?"

"Of course I do!" exclaimed Roberta, before adding, in a tone Lucía thought must be ironic, "When the bird's spirit escaped through its beak in the form of a soap bubble filled with smoke, and squeezed in through your mother's mouth . . ."

"Well, I never said it was the bird's spirit."

"What else could it have been?"

"You'd have to ask a theologian that" was the answer that came to Lucía.

Roberta laughed at this and, since they were about to arrive, she said that Lucía should hurry up and tell her the rest of the story of her mother's death.

"It was summer; school was out. It had been a very hot day, but when the sun went down, it grew slightly cooler, and my father told me to go and keep my mother company."

"Your mother was bedridden?"

"She was permanently sedated. I found that out, or worked it out, later on, joining the dots over time."

"Why was she sedated?"

"I think my father had realized she was a bird woman and was afraid that she might fly away."

Roberta laughed.

"Go on."

"So, I was at her bedside, observing her bird woman's nose, which had grown even longer and thinner while she'd been ill, when suddenly she sat up and cried out, 'Something's going to happen!' Immediately, a swallow flew in through the open window, did a very quick lap of the room, and flew back out again, clearing the window frame just as cleanly as when it had entered. My mother watched it all the way and, once it had gone, her head fell to one side and, with a smile on her face, she died."

"Sure you didn't make the swallow up?"

"Of course not."

Or did I? Lucía wondered.

In bed that night, again letting herself enter the fantasy of Roberta's being a reincarnation of her mother, her mind returned to thoughts of the age she had been when she lost her mother, and again she found a correspondence with what was now going on in her life: Roberta had, after all, appeared just as she was making the transition from one way of life to another. But the question was, Why? Perhaps to reveal to her that she, like her mother, was a bird woman, a state of being that she really ought to accept. Shrugging in the bed, she smiled at the thought of having a mission to fulfill. Then, excited at the idea of Roberta's testing her to see if she was worthy of this revelation and the responsibility it entailed, she got out of bed, went over to her computer, and typed into the browser "bird women."

Close to a million different results came up, related to arts of every kind (music, painting, dance . . .). But her eye was immediately drawn to an article on Wikipedia about a woman named Koo Koo, born in 1880 and living a life of poverty, who had been known as "Bird Girl." She had "a very short stature, a small head, a narrow birdlike face with a beaklike nose, large eyes, a receding

jaw, large ears, and a mild intellectual disability."
She had been used as a circus freak until, report-
edly, disappearing one day without anyone's having any proof she had died—as though she had
simply taken to the sky and never come back.
Lucía looked up photos of Koo Koo, whose obvious
frailty reminded her of her mother when she came
back from wherever she had gone away to, shortly
before dying in bed. It now struck Lucía that she
had never asked herself, or anyone else, what
the nature of that internment had been, and that
during it, given her mother's state when she came
back, her wings must surely have been clipped.

She went back to bed and fell asleep pondering
the happy idea that perhaps her mother belonged
to a world that was now beginning, for the first
time, to make contact with her.

ONE DAY, A LITTLE before lunchtime, after
taking a fare to Tirso de Molina and now on her
way out of the semigridlocked neighborhood, she
turned down a narrow street restricted to pedes-
trians and public transport, and came across a
tattoo parlor; some colorful flyers in the window
caught her eye. She left the car in a parking lot
nearby and went in to investigate.

The establishment seemed to her like a med-
ical clinic, an impression she found reassuring.

She was welcomed by a young woman in a white coat sitting behind a counter; her body was like a sampler of all manner of piercings and tattoos. A multicolored snake came up from between her breasts, twisting all the way up her throat and over her chin, its extended forked tongue stopping just short of a steel or silver ball on a piercing in her bottom lip. She also had a nose ring, an eyebrow ring, and some Japanese or Chinese characters down the right side of her neck. Her very short hair had alternating patches of blond and orange. She looked outwardly tough, but that melted away the moment she opened her mouth, since she had a gentle voice, while around her eyes, there remained something slightly guarded.

"I'm Raquel," she said, shaking Lucía's hand.

Lucía, still feeling slightly intimidated, said she was thinking about having a couple of words tattooed on her pubis. Hearing this, the girl moved her head in a way that seemed to suggest comprehension and doubt at the same time. Without directly advising against it, she showed her a picture of a body with the places most sensitive to the needle of the "artist"—as he was referred to—mapped on it. The pubis was a red zone, meaning it would hurt.

"But if it's important to you, he'll do it," she added.

"It's important," said Lucía.

"And what do you want the tattoo to be of?"

"Two words: *Nessun dorma.*"

"Hold on, I'll make a note."

"*Nessun,* with two *s*'s. *Dorma,* just the way it sounds."

"What does it mean?"

"'Let No One Sleep.' It's the name of an aria from *Turandot,* the Puccini opera."

"I know nothing about opera, but Armando loves it. I'll pass this on to him; then he'll have a look at different fonts to suggest, though in the end you'll be free to choose any you want."

Lucía waited for whatever might be required next, imagining other stages to the process; she had thought of having a tattoo as being like a surgical intervention, and now it all seemed too simple.

"Tuesdays are good for me," she said, since Raquel was saying nothing.

The young woman, consulting the computer, said, "Well, he's got a gap next Tuesday at eleven. Although the pubis hurts, at the same time it isn't a big tattoo you're asking for. Once you agree on the font, he'll have it done for you in no time."

Lucía was about to say good-bye and go out, when Raquel said she ought to have her pubis waxed.

"So one session will be enough?" asked Lucía.

"For those two words, yes. If you're having just one color."

"And is it possible to ask for a woman instead of—"

"It's only Armando working here, but don't worry, it's like going to the doctor's. He's really good, the best. He's done tattoos for all kinds of actresses and singers, in places you can't even imagine."

Lucía *could* imagine, in fact, having seen just such tattoos on the Internet, but she feigned surprise.

She came away feeling slightly confused, thinking she wouldn't keep the appointment, then that she would, and then changing her mind again and deciding that she wouldn't. But, back in the taxi once more, her mind turning to the fantasy encounter with the actor, and her presenting him with a gift of this kind, she decided again that she would. So, that same afternoon, she went into a beauty parlor to have her pubis waxed. The woman who saw to her was roughly her own age and quite mesmeric; because of the anesthetic properties of her conversation, the waxing didn't hurt nearly as much as on other occasions.

When she explained to the beautician that she was planning to have a tattoo there, and why, the woman roared with laughter and lowered her overalls to reveal a buttock with an enormous, brightly colored frog tattoo; the frog was shooting out its tongue to catch an insect, which had been intricately rendered on her coccyx. She told Lucía it had been a gift to her husband, who was a great enthusiast when it came to the microcosms of ponds, and for cold-blooded animals in general.

"I'm going to get an iguana on the other buttock, with the tail down the back of my thigh—to here, more or less." She pointed to the back of her knee. "It's being designed for me at the moment."

By coincidence, she, too, was due to have a tattoo by Armando, who, she assured Lucía, was the best around.

"You've got nothing to worry about. He'll do a great job."

She left the beauty parlor feeling much better about the whole thing, and when she got home, she spent a long time looking at fonts on the Internet. She couldn't decide whether it should be something ostentatious or austere, or if the letters should have a touch of color or be completely black. Before getting into bed, she took off her clothes, stood in front of the mirror, and, not without some difficulty, wrote the two magic words in black marker pen, one beneath the other, on her skin, which was still slightly red from the waxing:

Nessun

dorma

Clumsily written though they were, they gave her pubis a touch of mystery nobody could fail to find captivating. She then decided she would go for a more austere font, and that it would be in black only.

Just before she got into bed, she received a message from her ex-colleagues at the IT company. They had a group WhatsApp for sharing updates on the class-action lawsuit they were bringing against the company's owner; because he had filed fraudulently for bankruptcy, they had received neither their final month's pay nor the settlements they were owed. There was a meeting the following day with the labor lawyer who had taken on the case.

9

THE MEETING WITH the labor lawyer, which went on until after 8:00 P.M., did not go as anyone had hoped; he said that their chances of receiving anything at all were slim. Lucía's ex-colleagues also poked fun—though not openly—at her appearance. She shouldn't have gone with her Chinese makeup on; she was so used to it by now that it hadn't even occurred to her that people would notice.

The group left the lawyer's office, which was something of a dive, in low spirits. Nonetheless, someone suggested they go out for drinks, an invitation Lucía declined, primarily because she didn't feel like it, but also because her earnings had been down in recent days. She went back to the taxi resolved to work that night until she was too tired to carry on.

It wasn't so much a quiet night as anesthetic. To combat her boredom, and after dropping off a couple at a Chinese restaurant with lots of yellow lanterns outside the door, she imagined that she was driving her taxi through Beijing. To that end, she started turning down side streets and alleyways at random, the narrowest and darkest she came across, until she succeeded in becoming thoroughly lost. The sensation, stimulating and disturbing at the same time, made her forget all about the meeting with her former colleagues, which was even more unpleasant each time she thought back over it, and deposited her in Beijing— well, if not in Beijing itself, then in a place with the same quality of realness as the images that arise between sleeping and waking, when one is asleep but thinks one's awake, and vice versa.

Later, as the night wore on, the streets grew livelier and she had a couple of short runs that obliged her to return from her imaginary Beijing to the real-life Madrid. Later still, having lost her bearings once more, and without quite knowing how, she emerged onto Gran Vía, crowds of people out for the night packing the sidewalks. A Chinese woman had a stall outside the Telefónica building, where she was selling drinks, noodles, and fried rice. Without getting out of the car, Lucía bought some noodles and a bottle of water, then went back to her Beijing fantasy, reinforced now by the ambience of the streets around her.

She liked being in Beijing, it felt good there, and she therefore decided to turn on *Turandot,* the action of which unfolded in an older version of that great city, and again she let herself be taken along the back streets behind Gran Vía, looking for a place to have dinner. After advancing for ten or fifteen minutes like a lab rat in a maze, she pulled up by a blind alley, down which she could see a nightclub with Oriental motifs decorating the outside. She double-parked and was about to start on her noodles and recharge a little, when she heard the back door open and turned to find a man getting in, which appeared to be something of a struggle. Mumbling to her to take him to Manuel Becerra, he fell instantly asleep. All of this took place in the space of seven or eight seconds, possibly less.

Lucía gave up on her dinner, leaving the noodles on the passenger seat, turned on the meter, and pulled out, wondering to herself where this individual had sprung from. He had appeared seemingly out of thin air; she hadn't even noticed any shadows moving in her mirrors. She set off in the direction of Manuel Becerra—Manuel Becerra in Beijing, she should have said, since it seemed clear to her that the man, in his stupefied state, had just come out of an opium den. After four or five minutes, she took the opportunity of stopping at a red light to turn on the ceiling light and have a closer look at the man, wondering if he might be on death's door, or even dead already. And it was then that she recognized him: It was none other than the owner of the IT company, the man against whom she and her ex-colleagues were bringing their class-action suit. The asshole.

Something's going to happen, said the voice inside her head.

When the light turned green, she changed course and headed instead toward the outskirts of Beijing, without knowing very well where these might be, simply letting instinct guide her. Leaving the city center, she made her way down a regular-size street, which led to another set of backstreets, which, in turn, brought her out onto a ring road. After a short while on this, she came to another of the city ring roads, and then another. When she looked at the road signs, the letters and symbols began coming apart and rearranging themselves into Chinese characters, which she had no difficulty understanding, possessed as she was now by a lucidity that took her back to the stimulants she had consumed as a teenager. On she went into the suburbs, *Turandot* playing at full volume—inside the taxi and inside her head.

After half an hour, or perhaps forty-five minutes, she came to an area of open ground that lay in darkness except for a bonfire, around which, like ghosts silhouetted against the flames, a number of figures stood warming their hands. She stopped the car a prudent distance away, turned off the headlights, got out, opened the back door, and, taking the man by the jacket, dragged him out. He slumped to the ground, as if he were nothing but a sack containing bodily organs. Before fleeing the scene, on an impulse, she reached into his inside jacket pocket and took out his wallet. As she removed the money, the fleeting thought came to her of his cell phone, which could be used to track his journey from the center of Beijing to this lot on the outskirts. Throwing the wallet to the ground, she started going through the rest of his pockets, of which there were quite a few. But the zombies had already left the warmth of the bonfire and started to approach, and they were almost close enough by now to be able to make out her license plate. She got in as quickly as she could and drove off without turning on the headlights. The last thing she saw were the shadows of the homeless people leaning over her asshole of a former boss, like hungry animals over a piece of carrion.

She arrived home at 3:00 A.M. in a state of complete euphoria, and tried to bring herself back to earth by walking barefoot back and forth around the apartment. Her head was a calculator capable of carrying out several functions at the same time. She coolly thought back over what she had just done, how she had acted, and the likelihood of her being found out if the man, when he came around, went to the police. She organized all the data pertaining to what had happened in a list inside her mind, as in a flowchart:

- Given the state the man was in when he got into the taxi, the most likely thing is that he wouldn't even be able to remember what kind of car it was.

- Nor would he have noticed that it was a woman driving.

- She would have to go and check the blind alley where she'd stopped to eat her noodles, to see if there were any security cameras around, though you tended to get security cameras only outside of banks or big commercial premises, and there were neither anywhere near there.

Thousands of incidents like this must take place nightly in a city like Beijing, and at most the authorities would try to keep track of the numbers.

Then, while still moving around the apartment to give her excitement that physical outlet, she counted the money she'd taken from the man's wallet: 570 euros in all. It wasn't what the company owed her, but it was some recompense, moral recompense, and it made up for her poor earnings in recent days. She rolled up the bills and put them in a Ziploc bag, which she sealed and placed inside the freezer, where for a while she had been keeping a certain amount of cash in case there should be a run on the banks one day.

She undressed and got into her pajamas, but she quickly saw that sleep wasn't going to come, because she had a fever, not a fever that could be measured on any thermometer, as she wasn't ill, but a fever of a mental kind: Her mind was burning up, boiling over, as though her thoughts themselves had become exceptionally hot.

In reality, her mind had been burning up and boiling over ever since the day she'd found out that Braulio Botas was an actor. Her fear of not being up to his level conversationally when the day finally came that he'd get in her taxi (it was going to happen; it was written in the stars) had led her to read dozens of articles online about the world of theater, as well as the rare interview she could find with Botas that coincided with a play of his going up. And in every one of these she had discovered entire worlds, the existence of which she hadn't so much as suspected before. And every one of these worlds floated around in one or another room in her awareness, since this was how she imagined a person's awareness, like a set of rooms in which different ideas, or groupings of ideas, were developing, ideas that assembled in the living room at certain moments, joining together to form theories. The image was not her own, but Botas's: He had spoken about conceiving his research into his characters in precisely this way.

Ideas burned and boiled, then, inside her head. She had just come back from discovering Beijing, the modern version of the city in which Puccini's opera took place, and she had visualized, once, a thousand times, the square in which Princess

Turandot spurned her suitors, a wonderfully beautiful square, adorned with the impaled heads of those who had been rebuffed. There were dozens of birds flapping around, some dropping down to pluck out an eye or tear off part of one of the lips. It was quite common for her to see the square from the same perspective as the flock, because she herself was one of its number.

She then made up her mind never to leave Beijing again, and, similarly, that, sooner or later, she and the actor would find each other, just as two seemingly distinct ideas come together to create another, far-reaching idea. Impelled by all these different stimuli, she got out of bed, turned on the computer, typed "Beijing" into the browser, and started navigating around that city, going the length and breadth of it, availing herself of the abundance of color maps, some of which she also printed off to have in the taxi with her. Of course, in her feverish state, she had no difficulty finding the area on the outskirts where she had abandoned her former boss, that utter asshole who had, in effect, left her out in the street by denying her and her colleagues their rightful severance pay.

She got back into bed as the sun was coming up, but such was her ongoing mental energy that she still found it impossible to shut her eyes. She tossed and turned, while more and more thoughts spun and wheeled about, vertiginously, like swallows.

After two hours, having dropped in and out of the briefest of dreams—these were like short tunnels in her wakefulness—she jumped out of bed feeling completely refreshed, just as if she had slept eight or nine hours consecutively. She still felt unusually alert, so that as she had some coffee but nothing to eat (she wasn't the slightest bit hungry), she came up with an algorithm to correspond with her current situation, from which she surmised that her first step would be to go back to the blind alley and check for any cameras that might have captured the moment when the asshole had stepped into the taxi.

SHE LEFT THE TAXI in a nearby parking lot and made her way to the blind alley on foot, retracing the route she had driven in the early hours. The first CCTV camera she saw was five blocks from where she had picked the man up. All clear on that front. She guessed that he must have been in that particular neighborhood for the prostitutes, and that he was heading to Manuel Becerra to continue the bender in one of the seedy clubs there, given that his home was a mansion in a residential neighborhood on the outskirts.

She went back to the taxi and decided to go for a drive around the city center. Any time she had the chance, she always returned to the center. She supposed taxi drivers in general must have certain areas of the city to which they gravitated, and this, she had just learned, was hers.

She turned the radio on just as the news was starting. The announcer was saying that a man, identity as yet unknown, had been found dead in an empty lot near Madrid's illegal drug super-markets. The body, which had been naked, and on which there had been no ID or cell phone, was undergoing an autopsy by the forensic police.

For a few moments, Lucía couldn't breathe. At the thought of the asshole's cell phone's having dis-appeared—if indeed it was him—she found she was able to breathe again.

10

SHE DROVE DOWN TO the Cibeles Fountain, listening to the radio with bated breath, but after the news bulletin, the normal programming resumed. At the junction of Gran Vía and Alcalá, outside the Círculo de Bellas Artes, she was hailed by a woman with a large buggy, the kind designed for twins, with the two seats positioned facing each other, as though the pair were looking in a mirror. But only one of the seats had a child in it, a toddler, producing a somewhat disturbing asymmetry. She had to get out and help the woman fold the buggy up and lift it into the trunk; since the traffic was fairly heavy, this produced a certain amount of chaos in the street. Lucía, without being careless, helped the woman in a mechanical way, still reeling from the news of the dead body. Was it the man she had driven out to the Chinese dumping ground? She needed to know. The angst kept her feeling fully awake, in spite of a lack of sleep. In fact, she felt more than awake: lucid, full to bursting with mental energy.

The woman apologized for all the to-do, to

which Lucía said not to worry—after all, what were taxis for? The woman was going to calle Hiedra, near Plaza Castilla, and Lucía, partly as a game but partly with complete seriousness, checked the exact location on one of the maps of Beijing she had printed out in the night. Pretending to herself that she was following the map, while in fact following it—as though the two things were possible—she drove back down to Cibeles, around the roundabout with the fountain in the middle, and onto Paseo de Recoletos. The idea of being in Beijing and Madrid at the same time, or the mental capacity to skip from one city to the other in a matter of seconds, gave her a bracing sensation of power. In the future, no matter what she got up to in Spain, she would be able to take refuge in China, and vice versa.

Since the toddler was very quiet in his mother's arms, with her seat belt strapping both of them in, Lucía asked him, in the idiotic tone adults assume when addressing children, where he'd left his brother or sister.

The boy lowered his eyes, while the mother, looking at Lucía in the rearview mirror, silently mouthed the words *He's dead.*

Sorry! Lucía replied, also mouthing silently, eyebrows shooting up in surprise.

Her euphoria, without vanishing altogether, was certainly punctured. She felt exhausted, much like the subsiding of a fever after taking an antipyretic. But, she also noticed, it was a creative sort of flagging, similar to that which follows an intense orgasm—a momentary depression that allows for a clearer view of the world than the preceding exalted state. They were nearly at their destination when the toddler opened his mouth to speak.

"Mamá," he said, "did somebody die today?"

"Of course, sweetie, somebody dies every day." She said this while checking her watch, as though death were a thing that kept certain hours.

It was 10:50 A.M. The next news bulletin would be at 11:00 A.M. Fortunately, by 10:55 A.M. she had dropped off the woman and the solitary twin, and she was able to listen alone, with her heart, as the saying goes, in her mouth.

The body had been identified, and indeed it was that of her former boss. A man, the news report said, involved in various lawsuits pertaining to, among other crimes, fraudulent bankruptcies and embezzlement. The body, as well as having been stripped of its clothes, wallet, all documentation, and cell phone, showed signs of violence. The last person to have seen him alive was his secretary, who said he had left the office around 7:00 P.M., leaving his car in the garage and giving no indication of where he was going. After that, his trail went cold. No information had been forthcoming as to how he had ended up on the outskirts of the city, in the vicinity of one of the so-called drug superstores, or where he had been in the hours leading up to that. There was speculation, given the route he had taken, about a revenge killing, as well as the possibility that the murder had taken place elsewhere and the body had been dumped in the lot. In any case, the autopsy had revealed the presence of both alcohol and narcotics in his system.

Given the distance from the dead man's office to the place she had picked him up, and between those places and his home, Lucía had to imagine that he had decided against taking his car because of the bender he was planning, not wanting to drive home in such a state. If so, he had most likely taken a taxi from his office to the place where, in his semiconscious state, she had picked him up. The only links were that taxi driver and perhaps the club or brothel where he had gotten high. But nobody in his right mind, even if the person recognized the photos doubtless already being circulated on TV, would offer up the fact he had seen him. That would be asking for the kind of trouble that has a clear beginning but not such a clear end.

The lack of evidence concerning the dead man's movements during the night was clearly in Lucía's favor. She felt good, secure, pleased with herself— like all the pieces were in place. Messages soon started arriving on her ex-colleagues' WhatsApp. She did nothing more than acknowledge the news, though she would have liked to see people's faces had they learned of her part in the whole thing.

Her homing instinct was taking her back to the center when, passing Cuzco subway station, she was hailed by a couple, a man and a woman in their fifties. When they got in, they were having an argument over the length of jacket sleeves, and they went on arguing once they had given Lucía the address they were going to.

"If all the sleeves on all the jackets are too long on you," said the husband with an air of finality, "it probably means you've got short arms. Sleeves can be adjusted; arms can't."

The woman thanked him sarcastically before plunging into a silence that seemed more disconsolate than hostile, while the man, pleased that she had withdrawn from the field, made himself comfortable in the seat, a victorious look on his face. The sleeves of jackets and shirts often were too long on Lucía's arms also, meaning she took the man's pronouncement as a slight against her, as well.

"Worse to have a wagging tongue than short arms," she said, looking the man in the eye in the rearview mirror.

"What did you say?" blurted the man.

He didn't know he was talking to the same woman who, just a few hours before, had played a role in wiping an out-and-out son of a bitch from the face of the earth. Lucía felt there was nothing she was incapable of.

"I said, if I were your wife, I'd have given you a couple of slaps with those hands she's got at the end of her short arms."

A minute then passed with nobody saying anything. Driving around silently for sixty whole seconds, possibly a little more, with the mounting tension inside the car, created an extreme sense of violence, which Lucía greatly enjoyed. She felt so powerful, so strong, that she almost wished the man would come out with one more tactless remark, just so that she could stop the car, turn around, and give him a slap herself. But he said nothing, though he was white with fury. Doubtless he could tell the taxi driver was a natural-born killer capable of absolutely anything. After that long, slow minute, and though they were not yet at their destination, the man, trying to claw back a modicum of dignity, finally opened his mouth.

"Just drop us here."

"My pleasure," said Lucía, slamming on the brakes.

Then, when the man went to get his money out of his wallet, she said he should stick it up his ass. Instead of this, the man took out a ten-euro bill, threw it down in the footwell, and silently got out, followed by his wife.

After picking up the bill, Lucía drove on to Gran Vía, which she drove the length of without passing a single person trying to hail a cab. At Plaza de España, she turned onto calle Ferraz without any particular idea of where she was going. She was hungry, but it was early to stop for lunch. When you drive a taxi, eating early can make the second half of the day go on forever.

She then fielded two calls from the taxi company, a couple of short runs: the first for a little over twelve euros, the second for eight euros. At 2:00 P.M., at the corner of Alberto Aguilera and Galileo, her cell phone rang, an unknown caller. She answered it using her hands-free device. A man asked if she could pick him up in twenty minutes on calle Almirante. Lucía checked the clock and said she would be there, setting off for the given address. Her insistence on handing out those business cards was starting to pay off.

He was a well-turned-out man of forty or forty-five. Slim, rather tall, wearing a brown cashmere sweater and matching scarf, he had a hooked nose—another bird man. She couldn't remember having seen him before, and supposed that one of her many satisfied customers must have given him her number. In any case, she felt it would be inappropriate to ask.

Once he was in and had given her the address, Lucía put *Turandot* on at a low volume, trying to seem interesting. She had gone with the ballerina's bun that day, leaving the nape of her neck bare. The man took the bait.

"Do you like opera?" he asked.

"I *try* to like it," she said.

This disconcerted him somewhat, or so it seemed to Lucía, but he quickly recovered. He was no fan of opera, he said, and he had no problem admitting it.

"I just find it unconvincing," he said. "All those overweight singers playing thin people, all those tenors with their big puffed-up chests . . . To me, it's all just funny. Even during the most dramatic moments, I can't help but laugh. No disrespect."

"To each his own," said Lucía, as if it made no difference what he thought. "But, tell me, have you ever listened closely to birdsong?"

"Honestly, no. I do listen to the birds, but not very closely."

"If you did, and you knew a little bit about opera, you would see that a lot of sopranos, when they sing, though they're still using words, are actually warbling like birds. And in those moments, the important thing isn't the words, which are almost impossible to understand, but what the *warbling* is saying."

"And how do you come to know all this?"

"I know because I'm a bird woman," she said, smiling at him in the rearview mirror. She delivered this with a completely straight face.

"So what do they say in the warblings?"

"Nobody knows. Nobody's ever deciphered birdsong."

"But you, being a bird woman, ought to know."

"If I do, I'm not telling."

"Well, you should."

"I'll give you an example. Maria Callas. She was a bird woman. You only had to look at her side-on when she was singing. Have you ever heard of Yma Sumac?"

"No."

"She was a Peruvian contralto; she's dead now, but she learned to imitate birdsong."

"And was she a bird woman, as well?"

"Look up pictures of her face online, then listen to her singing, and you can decide for yourself. By the way, you look like a bird man, but from what I can see, not the temperament."

"I can't tell you how sorry I am about that."

"Me, too."

"And what is this we're listening to?"

"*Turandot,* by Puccini."

"Puccini, ah, yes. What's it about?"

"A Chinese princess whose name is Turandot, whom all the princes in the world want to marry, although she doesn't want to marry any of them. So she sets them each three riddles, saying she'll marry whomever gets them right. But the ones who don't get them right are beheaded at dawn, and their heads are put on spikes around the main square, in sight of the whole city."

"What a show!"

"And the birds of Peking fly around above the

heads of the living and the dead, filling the air with cawing and warbling. Sometimes they fly down to peck out the eyes of the dead. Or the tongues, once they're done with the noses and the lips."

"Like I say, quite the show!"

"One of those birds," said Lucía unexpectedly, as though not of her own volition, "is my mother. My mother warbles, or trills, in fact, because she's a swallow."

The passenger was as perplexed as Lucía was by this.

"Sorry," she said, after bursting into laughter to try to defuse the strange moment, "but the thing is, just before my mother died, I went into her bedroom and a swallow flew in through the window, and my mother, who had a fever and was delirious, said the swallow was her. I mean, that memory just came to me out of the blue. But we were talking about Turandot, the Chinese princess in the Puccini opera."

"Yes," said the man, "you told me she set her suitors three riddles. What were they, then?"

"If I tell you, and you get them right, you'll have to marry me. But if you don't, well . . ." She smiled in the rearview mirror, drawing her thumb across her throat.

The man pretended to hesitate.

"Why does Turandot hate men?" he asked.

"Oh, old stuff, family stuff," said Lucía. "And

because men, no offense, are generally slightly despicable."

"More than just slightly, surely," he said, giving an actorly smile.

"You said it, not me."

A few seconds passed without either of them saying anything. It was as if they were playing chess. In the end, he selected a piece and made his move.

"And do you wear that makeup because you identify with the Chinese princess?"

"I'm the real Chinese princess," said Lucía, beaming. "The one in the opera is made up."

They were starting to enjoy themselves, although Lucía could have sworn he was having a better time than she.

"Okay, then, hit me with the riddles."

"You know what you're getting into, though— marriage or death."

"I hope it's worth it. What's the first one?"

"Listen carefully: 'In the gloomy night, an iridescent phantom flies. It spreads its wings and rises over infinite humanity. Everyone invokes it; everyone implores it. But the phantom disappears at dawn to be reborn in the heart. And every night it's born and every day it dies.'"

The man contemplated Lucía, a little taken aback at the passion of her recital.

"I have no idea," he said, though rather too quickly.

"Hope!" exclaimed Lucía. "Isn't that lovely? . . . It spreads its wings and rises over infinite humanity! . . . And every night it's born and every day it dies."

Repeating it made her feel slightly emotional, and the man, quite moved in turn, then asked for the second riddle.

"Here goes," said Lucía. "'It flickers like flame, and is not flame. Sometimes it rages. It's feverish, impetuous, burning. But idleness changes it to languor. If you're defeated or lost, it grows cold. If you dream of winning, it flames. Its voice is faint, but you listen; it gleams as bright as the sunset.'"

"Beats me!" said the man.

"Blood!" cried Lucía.

"Well, since I'm already condemned to die, tell me the third."

"'Ice that sets you on fire and from your fire is more frosty. White and dark. If she sets you free, she makes you a slave. If she accepts you as a slave, she makes you a king.'"

"I don't know."

"Turandot!"

"Turandot? Are you ice that sets on fire? Whom do you set on fire, if I might ask?"

"Calaf. Do you know who Calaf is in the opera? He's the only prince she falls for, thereby going against a whole tradition of hating men."

"And may I ask who Calaf is in real life?"

"In real life, he calls himself Braulio Botas, and he's an actor."

"Ah, I know who he is. But he doesn't work very much; he must live off his wife. In fact, I think they separated a few months ago, but they got back together. She, if I'm not mistaken, is an anthropologist. She was on TV once, talking about Atapuerca."

Lucía was expressionless as she received this information. So, Braulio was with someone, but they had separated for a number of months (the time he was living in Lucía's building, no doubt), and he possibly lived off her because his theater work paid badly. An anthropologist.

"Not that there's anything between him and me," Lucía said, clarifying the situation. "I don't even know him, but I admire him greatly." Then, to move the conversation away from the subject of Botas, which she now wished she hadn't brought up, she asked, "And what line of work are you in?"

"I'm a writer."

"Oh, really, what do you write?"

"I write . . . novels," he said, his hesitation not lost on Lucía. "And I write for newspapers."

"You write about culture and you don't like opera?"

"Oh, nothing like that. Economics, business journalism. Well, you have to turn your hand to everything nowadays, but I like economic data."

"Way over my head!"

"Don't you believe it. Want to know how it works?"

"Sure."

"Well, I take an article, any article, I zoom in a little bit or I zoom out, to freshen it up a little, make it seem novel, even though I've copied it from somewhere else. Some days, all journalists covering economics write the same article in all the papers. Although they might seem different, if you look closely, you'll see they aren't at all. We get paid the same for trotting out other people's ideas as when we come up with one of our own."

"So cynical! But to my mind, because of our egos, we can't help but want to do things well."

"Oh, completely. One way of doing things well is to avoid current events. Or to make them not current. Making current events not current is very similar to making a stuffed onion."

"What a box of tricks you are. What's the recipe?"

"You empty out the inside of the onion, being careful not to let the whole thing fall apart, leaving just one or two layers, the outermost ones, obviously. You sauté the onion you've emptied out along with some chopped pepper, tomato, and garlic. Add cider or white wine and bring it to a boil, then let it reduce so you end up with a thick sauce, which, if you season it nicely, will be very tasty. Then put a can of tuna in, because canned food always makes things not current, fry it a little bit to get all the different flavors to mingle, then fill the empty onion with all of that, and put the filled onion in the oven until it turns golden brown. The end result, to the taste, is the same as if you'd just fried it all together. The secret is in the shape: A filled onion is a not-current onion. You work with other people's articles in a similar way: empty out the current information while respecting the outermost layer, et cetera."

This guy, thought Lucía, may have known nothing about Turandot, but he does know Chinese. And she told him so.

"You speak Chinese. What you've just told me wasn't off the cuff; you've come up with it as a way of seducing simple people like myself."

The man looked at the clock and said it was time to eat.

"Since you're not allowed to behead me," he said, smiling, "would you at least let me buy you a drink?"

"It would need to be in a Chinese restaurant," she said. "I got out of bed today feeling like I was working in Beijing."

11

THEY WEREN'T FAR from Legazpi now, and the man said there was a Chinese restaurant there that Asian people always ate at, a sure sign that it was the real deal.

"They do an amazing lobster in ginger sauce," he said. "The problem is going to be parking."

"Don't worry about that," said Lucía. "There's a public parking lot right there."

From the moment she had accepted his invitation, a tension had grown inside the taxi, generated by his hopes, or expectation, of a conquest. For her part, it was not that she didn't share those same hopes, but they worked on her without the same urgency she discerned in him. As a consequence, the conversation ebbed in intensity, and the man began observing Lucía's bare nape and her face, side-on, with an air of appraisal. His eyes traveled across the parts of her body visible from where he was sitting (her right shoulder, her arms, and her hands on the steering wheel) like someone calculating the weight or quality of some merchandise. Just the way it always is, she thought.

When they got to the parking lot and Lucía told him the fare, the man went to pay with his credit card, but as he was about to hand it over, he retracted it, saying he would pay in cash.

"That's classy!" she said.

"What do you mean?" he replied, flustered.

"Leaving no trace?"

"What are you saying?"

"I'm saying this is a taxi, not a brothel. Even if your wife goes through your receipts, she won't find anything out of the ordinary."

The man said nothing, but he flushed bright red as he took out a fifty-euro note.

"Haven't you got anything smaller?"

"I haven't, I'm sorry."

"Okay, well you're going to clear me out of change. It doesn't matter, but just get it into your head that you're paying for the taxi ride, not anything else."

"Sure, I know that."

"Just checking."

They got out of the car and, when the elevator didn't come, took the stairs. When they got up to street level, in spite of the cold, the sun was dazzling. As they made their way to the restaurant, the man apologized about the credit card.

"It was just a reflex," he said.

"Quite the reflexes you've got there! What's your name? If you want, you can make one up."

"Ricardo. Really."

"And your wife?"

"My wife's got nothing to do with anything."

Lucía noted Ricardo growing increasingly cold the closer they got to the restaurant.

"Cat's got your tongue," she said. "If you aren't in the mood, let's just leave it. Look, since you've got my number, you can call me some other time—when you need a ride. And if you've got time then, I'll take you for something to eat."

The man stopped walking.

"I think you're being nasty to me because I like you."

"It isn't because you like me," she said. "People always like me; I'm used to that. It's because when you got the slightest sniff of sex, you turned cheap. Sex makes some men generous, and other men cheap. It turned you cheap."

"Shall we leave it, then?

"Sure, let's leave it."

"Nice to have met you."

They shook hands, turned, and went their separate ways.

It's almost better this way, she thought. She had discerned in Ricardo some vague threat, a dark edge from which she had been saved, thanks perhaps to the buildup of tiredness over the past few hours, which was starting to manifest in her mood. She went back to the taxi and aimed for home, deciding not to stop for anyone who wasn't going her way.

At the second traffic light she came to, a woman got in, asking to go to the airport. It wasn't what Lucía had been expecting, but a run to the airport was always worth one's while. Soon after they were under way, Lucía was momentarily distracted, and an obstacle in the road meant she had to brake suddenly. The woman asked her to drive carefully.

"Don't your nerves ever get a bit frayed?" asked Lucía.

"Jesus Christ helps my nerves not to get frayed," said the woman.

Lucía realized that the woman had been looking for a chance to bring up Jesus Christ since she'd gotten into the taxi. Some people were like this. Others felt the need to tell you they were surgeons or disc jockeys on the radio. She had a gentle, deliberate, slightly hypnotic way of speaking, a way of impressing upon her interlocutor the miracle of her merely having opened her mouth. She was conscious of every word she spoke, in the way that an ex-smoker, giving way to temptation, is conscious of every single drag. Like she'd been reborn.

"I've been reborn," the woman then said, reading Lucía's mind. "I used to be edgy all the time. I was so anxious, I'd get coughing fits."

"You're an evangelical," ventured Lucía.

"Yes, young lady, I belong to an evangelical church."

A succinct version of her story went like this:

She'd once had a dream that she had to give fifty euros to someone who was truly in need. Since this wasn't an exorbitant amount for a person of her means, and the dream was an unusually intense one, she decided to do as it bid her. For this, she went to an evangelical church close to where she lived, where on that day of the week food and clothes were handed out to people in dire straits, and she asked the man who seemed to be in charge whom she ought to give the donation to.

"Wait here a moment," he told her.

The woman stood watching what was going on, the food being handed out, and felt moved by the discretion of the people involved in this act of solidarity. After a short while, the director, or whatever the man was, came back.

"Here," he said. "Give it to this man."

The woman gave it to the person indicated, who, after taking the bill, hugged her and thanked her as though she had just saved his life. That embrace freed her from the demons of anxiety she had always carried inside her. So she said. And the cough, too. It wrought a mysterious change in her life.

Lucía felt touched by the story, but it did nothing to take away her own nerves, or her hunger pangs.

"Come see us one Saturday," said the woman as she was getting out, handing Lucía a card, which she put in the glove compartment.

Back home, and coming to count the day's takings, she found the fifty-euro bill Ricardo, the business journalist, had given her, and she decided that she, too, would give it to someone who was in great need. And then, who knew, perhaps she would finally have her moment with Braulio Botas on account of her good deed.

She went to the fridge, ate the first thing she laid her hands on, and fell asleep on the sofa, running through everything that had happened in the preceding few hours like someone going along a hallway with doors on either side. She was amazed at how many doors there were.

12

THE TUESDAY OF HER TATTOO came around—Tuesday's being her rest day. A hundred times she had decided she would not keep the appointment. And a hundred times that she would. Then another hundred times that she wouldn't. There were moments when the pros and cons mingled and combined in such a way that it was not always easy to distinguish one from the other.

It was a very damp morning, with a fine, misty rain leaving the bodywork of all the vehicles covered in what looked like a grainy sort of polish. Lucía usually dedicated Tuesday morning to the taxi's deep clean; she took it to a particular car wash, one frequented by other taxi drivers, both because it was very reasonable and because they practically disinfected the vehicles. If you stinted on cleaning, in four days your taxi would become a trash can, given the simple fact that people were not very clean. They were neither clean nor good nor considerate nor respectful. Generally, people were pretty disgusting. In fact, just the previous day she had picked a man up on the corner of calle

Velázquez and López de Hoyos, and no sooner had he gotten in than he had started picking his nose. He was wearing a suit and he smelled good, but he was also a snot rooter. Lucía glared at him in the rearview mirror, in the hope he would get the message. But this, far from shaming him, seemed to spur him on. In the end, she couldn't contain herself.

"Some people have no thought for the person after."

"What's that?" he said, removing his finger from his nostril.

"There are people who get in the taxi and leave it in the most despicable state, with no thought for the person who's going to get in next. I would ask you to kindly stop picking your nose."

Fortunately, the man did as he was asked, because she was quite prepared to kick him out of the taxi. But the tension that then installed itself did ruin the rest of that ride.

The memory came to Lucía of a trip she had taken to Barcelona once, when she was still working in programming. The man sitting next to her on the airplane had blown his nose and left the used Kleenex in the seatback. Lucía remembered the mother of one of her colleagues, who worked as a cleaner on airplanes, and thought about her inadvertently putting her hand on the dirty Kleenex. This, in turn, evoked a stock phrase of her father's: "Nobody thinks about the person after." She had heard it so many times, she had internalized it in such a way that she *only* thought of the person after. Perhaps that was why she had ended up driving taxis, so that she could think about the person after. She always left public bathrooms cleaner than when she had gone in, she recycled, and she never stuck gum under tabletops. She wondered if any of the people who came after her appreciated the effort she went to to make their lives easier.

When the man next to her in the airplane went to the bathroom, she took the Kleenex and put it inside an airsickness bag. Although she executed this as hygienically as she could, using only the tips of her forefinger and thumb, when the man came back, she went to wash her hands. Predictably enough, he had left the bathroom in a state, so she also cleaned that to leave it presentable for whomever came next. She then washed her hands, returned to her seat, and thought about how her father had tried to leave life clean for whomever came next, which was her, his daughter, but she doubted whether he had succeeded in his aim. Thinking of her father, and soothed by the roar of the airplane engine, she closed her eyes and fell asleep until they made a bumpy landing at their destination. She awoke to find her seatmate picking his nose.

So it wasn't a day for cleaning the car, given that it would only get dirty again in the smog-filled rain of the capital. She felt better that the weather had made the decision for her, and at 11:00 A.M. sharp, she walked through the door of the tattoo parlor, outwardly far calmer than she actually felt. Armando, the tattoo artist, immediately came out to welcome her; he was slim, about fifty years old, and had a silver eyebrow ring and his hair gelled up in a quiff, or crest, dyed various bright colors.

After she had signed the authorization slip given to her by the receptionist, Raquel, Lucía was led through to the back by Armando, who showed her the lettering he had chosen for her "Nessun dorma." It was a very simple font that looked handwritten.

"The simpler, the better," said Armando. "You don't want to be spending hours working on such a sensitive area."

He suggested that, rather than placing one word above the other, as had been Lucía's idea, he put them alongside each other, skirting the lower part of her mons veneris. He showed her the sample he had prepared on a piece of tracing paper. Lucía said yes, because at that moment, she would have said yes to anything, like a patient who has gone into surgery to have a tumor removed and is utterly bewildered by the fear and the sight of a space so alien.

The room was completely white, an antiseptic sort of white, and there were no windows, though it was brightly lit, with lights that were also white coming from everywhere and nowhere. Frightened as she was, everything appeared to her as separate and fragmented: on one side, the bed she was going to have to lie on; on the other, the little wheelie table bearing the inks, and then the tattoo artist's chair, the lamp, the electric pen. There seemed to be a smell of disinfectant, but all she smelled and saw was entirely out of keeping with the sounds she was hearing, which were the cries of a parrot in a very large cage in one corner. The parrot was welcoming the new arrival.

The parrot had a quiff, or crest, that looked like a copy of the tattoo artist's.

Armando smiled at Lucía's surprise, and went and placed a cloth over the cage to make the creature quiet down.

"He doesn't normally make such a racket," he said. "There's the screen for you to change behind. Take your clothes off and put the gown on—it's over there."

"Take everything off?"

"Pants and panties is fine. And your jacket, obviously. I don't know about the sweater; see what you think. As long as you can get the gown on comfortably, that's the main thing."

The hospital-like gown was a kind of blue poncho made of disposable fabric; it came halfway down her thighs and had ties to tighten it on the sides.

"Have you shaved completely?" asked Armando from the other side of the screen.

"Yes," said Lucía.

Once on the bed, she relaxed, in part thanks to the fact that Armando started to chatter about nothing in particular; though he was addressing her, really he was talking to himself. Lucía wondered if maybe it was a way to make the patients (the patients?) think that, because they were excluded from the conversation, they were not actually there in that place, baring their genitalia to a total stranger.

Something's going to happen, said her mother inside her head.

"It's best if you look at the ceiling," he said. "I've got a surprise for you."

He took a remote control from somewhere and pointed it at a stereo, at which the opening strains of *Turandot* immediately started to play. Lucía started to sob silently, her tears serving to release the tension that had been building up in her ever since she had decided she would, after all, keep the appointment. As she cried, or passively allowed the tears to fall, she felt Armando gently palpating her mons veneris, as though assessing the consistency of that part of her. Now, she thought, he will do the stencil I saw people doing on YouTube. She then imagined Braulio Botas also listening to *Turandot* that inclement, tear-filled morning, and let herself drift into a relaxed sort of numbness that gradually spread across her whole body.

Something's going to happen, said her mother inside her head.

"AM I HURTING YOU?" asked Armando.

"It's *Turandot* that really hurts," she said, almost adding that it was a curative pain.

"Try to think of something pleasant; I'm nearly done."

"Do you believe in coincidence?" Lucía asked.

"Why do you ask?"

"Because everything interesting has started happening for me this year, just when I've gotten to the age my mother was when she died."

"Well, I don't know. I'm more of a believer in meaning than in coincidence." He was trying to focus on his work.

"Meaning in what sense?"

"What's behind a tattoo. You must know."

Neither of them spoke for the rest of the session. Lucía was surprised to find she enjoyed the pain, and she lay looking up at the ceiling, picking out the shadows of various birds. There came a point when she was fully immersed in trying to discern these shapes, and she then heard Armando speaking, as if from a very long way off.

"That's it, all done. Just rest for a little bit before getting up. I'm going to uncover the parrot."

From where she lay, Lucía could hear the bird

again; it said, "Good morning" when the sheet was taken off. Armando spoke briefly with the creature, and while he did so, his profile and that of the parrot looked, in Lucía's eyes, practically identical.

"You two could be related," she said.

"Who told you we aren't? Anyway, you can get up now; just go slow."

Lucía sat up, with Armando's assistance.

"Okay, so I've put some antibacterial cream on, and a dressing over that, to avoid infections. Make sure you leave it on for at least twelve hours, and after that, you should wash the tattoo with lukewarm water. Once you're dressed, I'll give you a piece of paper with some instructions to follow over the coming days. You need to wear paper panties and protect the area with some sterile gauze. Whatever you do, don't let yourself scratch. If it's stinging, uncover it, get a hair dryer and dry it out, and try to leave it uncovered—let it have some air— for an hour a day. That'll help."

13

ROBERTA CALLED A NUMBER of days later to book Lucía for a job. She needed to be picked up midmorning that coming Thursday at the theater company's office in Callao, driven to the neighboring city of Toledo, and brought back to Madrid after lunch.

"I don't want this one going on the meter," she said. "Give me a price up front. I've also got a surprise for you."

As soon as she got in the taxi, Lucía told her about having had the tattoo done.

"Really?" said Roberta.

"I thought I'd told you about it. I got the words *Nessun dorma*—the aria from *Turandot* you already know about—in lettering that looks like it's been handwritten. It's a real work of art."

Roberta laughed, looking at Lucía in the rearview mirror as though she were pulling her leg.

"I don't believe it."

"You'd better."

"You're going to have to show me."

"You should be so lucky. It's a present for Braulio; it's for his eyes only."

"Has it happened yet? Have your paths crossed?"

"No, but it's written in the stars."

"For now, the only thing that's written is 'Nessun dorma.'"

"And that. There's no rush."

Roberta was busy the rest of the way, poring over some documents in a folder and having work conversations on her cell phone. From time to time, she shot Lucía an apologetic look.

"You don't stop," Lucía said at one point.

"That's how it is in this job; you have to take it or leave it."

"If you ever need an assistant, you know where I am."

"I promised you," Roberta said as they were arriving in Toledo, "that I had a surprise for you, but actually there are two. The first is that we are going to Rojas, the Toledo theater, meaning you can have a look at a set with nobody around, and imagine Braulio Botas walking the boards. It's really beautiful; you'll see—late 1900s, really well conserved. We invested a lot in a production that didn't come off, and it's my job to salvage whatever I can from the shipwreck. I thought we might as well take advantage."

"And the second surprise?"

"All in good time."

They went in through a side entrance, which

brought them into a hallway leading to the dressing rooms and the backstage area. Lucía, who felt overwhelmed by the ambience of the place, asked what the smell was.

"It's the smell of everything that goes into fabricating reality: paint, wood, sawdust, old cloth, dust, plumbing, makeup, oil for lubrication, shampoo, dye, even oxygen, secondhand oxygen, obviously. Can't you tell?"

"I didn't know there was such a thing as secondhand oxygen."

"Second-*lung* oxygen, to be exact. Well, now you know."

While Roberta went through to the offices, arguing over an inventory with the woman who had let them in, Lucía went and had a look around the dressing rooms, some of which had their own en suite bathrooms. Was there something uterine about all of this, with the twisting passageways that led from these backstage cells and hollows to the stage itself?

Sitting in front of a mirror with white lightbulbs around it, like the ones she'd seen so many times in movies, she carefully touched up her Turandot makeup, neatened her hair, which was gathered on the left side of her head that day, and went out to the hallway, the sheer quantity of silence contained inside the building pressing down intimidatingly on her. She went from one side to the other, as though passing along the cavities of a whale's belly. This image had come to her, that of the whale's belly, out of the blue, but it was reinforced upon her reaching the stage and looking out from the proscenium across the stalls and private boxes. The great horseshoe-shaped emptiness resembled a gigantic rib cage, with a phantasmal audience peeking in through the gaps, watching her every move.

She imagined a scene played by Braulio Botas before a rapt audience, a monologue interrupted by her when she walked onto the stage by mistake, having taken a wrong turn when trying to find her seat. The actor stopped what he was doing and turned to the intruder.

"What's going on?" he asked her.

"So sorry," she said. "I was trying to get to my seat, and I went the wrong way."

The audience, not completely sure whether this was an accident or part of the show, burst into laughter, rewarding the surprise with applause. Seeing what a hit the intrusion had proved, the actor went over to Lucía with a hand outstretched, inviting her to join him at center stage.

"Well, since you're here . . ."

Mortified, she went toward him, waving to the delighted audience, whom Botas then addressed.

"This is one of those curious moments in which life seeps into fiction."

Then, pointing to Lucía, he exclaimed, "Here you have life! And addressing you now is fiction."

And then, turning to Lucía once more, he asked, "What does life have to say to fiction?"

"If it's all the same to you," she said, "I'd rather tell you what fiction would say to life."

"Go for it."

"It would say, 'Where are you going in such a hurry?'"

The audience burst into peals of laughter, and Lucía imagined Braulio Botas, in that same instant, being struck by the fact that the woman before him was his perfect artistic match. Together, they would perform at all the theaters of the known world, using this same winning opening every time, followed by a plot in which it gradually became clear that the pair onstage were in fact Turandot and Calaf, the princess and the one prince in existence capable of answering her three riddles. It would close with the two of them in each other's arms and "Nessun dorma" blasting out at full volume.

She was taking in the applause from the imaginary audience as it rang around the packed theater, when she heard Roberta calling to her—for the fourth or fifth time.

"Sorry," she said. "I was imagining being in a play."

"You on your own?"

"No, me and Braulio Botas."

Since she never kept anything from Roberta, she told her what she had been imagining.

"Well, it isn't bad as an opening."

"Or as an ending—if you ask me."

"There's just the problem of the bit in between. But the idea of two of the most famous characters in a Puccini opera managing to get lost somehow, and then bumping into each other on a stage somewhere in the world . . . there's something to it."

"You really like it?"

"Sure, girl, I like it. But I'll like it even more after we've had lunch. We're all done here, and I'm famished. But before that, the second surprise I promised you."

Roberta went backstage and returned with a large handmade birdcage. Inside it was a bird with black plumage all over.

"Here, it's for you."

Lucía covered her mouth with her hands. It looked almost identical to the bird she had been given on her tenth birthday, her inseparable companion from that moment until the day it disappeared, ten years later. In fact, she had never wanted to have another bird because it had seemed so irreplaceable.

"It's the same as . . ." she began, choked with emotion.

"I know," said Roberta. "You gave me such a clear description of the other one. Although you never told me what became of it."

"It flew out of the window when I was twenty. I always assumed it had left to go and fly into the head of another woman like my mother. Where did you get this one?"

"It was part of the set design in the play we've just taken down. I thought that rather than give it back to the pet shop, I'd give it to you."

In tears, Lucía threw her arms around Roberta.

"You don't know what this means to me," she said once she had calmed down.

"Yes, I do. That's why I did it."

THEY HAD LUNCH AT El Parador, which had magnificent views over the city.

"It looks like a set," murmured Lucía, astonished.

When they were about to be seated, she went back to the taxi, having left the bird in the trunk. Though the day wasn't hot, she was worried about it running out of air. She left it at the hotel reception desk, asking the person there to avoid moving the cage suddenly or knocking it. During this brief interlude, meditating on the bond she had established with Roberta, it occurred to her that perhaps friendship prospered only in chance situations, the kind of situations taxis naturally seemed to bring about.

Joining Roberta in the restaurant, she said straightway, "I'm happy in my work. I've met you because of it, and I got my childhood bird back because of it."

"By the way," said Roberta, "I will need the cage back. It's included in the inventory, and it cost a fortune."

"Don't worry, I've still got Calaf's."

"Calaf's?"

"My first bird was called that."

"You never cease to amaze."

"And I'm a great driver. Right?"

"Sure. But don't you find it hard work, such long hours at the wheel?"

"No, because I imagine I'm driving in Beijing, and Beijing is a city you never tire of."

"You're crazy."

The two women exchanged glances, which, had they gone on a moment or two longer, would have turned into something meaningful, but then the maître d' arrived.

"For a first course, and given the cold weather," he began, at Roberta's request, "I recommend the garlic soup, which we make here unlike anywhere else. Then, as you know, the traditional cuisine of Toledo is game. Today we have a magnificent partridge stew."

There was an uncomfortable silence, eventually broken by Lucía. "I don't eat birds," she said, her eyes firmly fixed on her plate.

Roberta managed to resolve the situation in her usual relaxed manner, saying they would both have the same: garlic soup to start and some grilled fish as a main course.

When the maître d' went away, Lucía apologized for the scene. Talk of the partridge paved the way for her telling Roberta about an episode from her childhood, the day after her tenth birthday.

"It was a Monday," she said. "My father took me to school, but my mother came to pick me up. I saw her out of one of the windows as I was coming down the stairs. You could spot her a mile away with the dressing on her head after the ten stitches. She was talking to the father of a kid from a different grade, someone we never usually had anything to do with. Until that day, the two of them would have greeted each other like all the parents did, 'Good afternoon,' but that was all. I could tell from her gestures that my mother was telling him what had happened the day before, while the man nodded along. The curious thing is that this man had a very long, thin face, so that his eyes weren't on the same plane as the rest of his features. Like a bird, in other words. I had noticed him a few times before my mother's accident, but now, seeing him talking to her, my worries about the previous night came back. What if the smoke-filled soap bubble I'd seen passing from the bird's beak into my mother's mouth had *not* been my imagination? I went the rest of the way down the stairs, got to the schoolyard, and ran over, and when they saw me coming, they changed the subject. Before saying good-bye, he gave her a business card, which she put in her purse. 'Why were you talking to that man?' I asked her once we were in the car. He had just asked what happened to her head, she said—"

"Stop!" said Roberta. "You're making it all up!"

Am I? Lucía wondered.

"Later on," she continued, "I found out that the man owned a pet shop, actually the place where they'd gotten my birthday bird."

"You're crazy," said Roberta once more, affectionately, before bursting into laughter.

Lucía had never known what a seductive storyteller she was.

Roberta also spent the journey back working nonstop, looking certain documents over, talking on her cell phone. As they were getting back into Madrid, Lucía suggested they stop by her apartment to put the bird in Calaf's old cage, so Roberta could take the other one with her.

"It would be the most practical thing," agreed Roberta. "Then you can take me to the office; I've got about a million emails I need to answer."

Lucía sensed that Roberta was keen to see inside her apartment, and when they went up, she looked around in the same way Lucía had looked around the theater, seemingly in expectation of some marvel.

"It's really nicely done, very tidy," said Roberta.

"Thank you."

"Cozy, too."

"Do you really think so?"

"Sure."

"Living on my own, it's more than enough. Come this way; I'm going to show you the bathroom."

Roberta followed her.

"What's so special about it?"

"The air vent. It's where I used to hear *Turandot* coming in, when Braulio Botas was living downstairs."

"This vent deserves to be in a museum of love," said Roberta.

"Don't joke. I'd have it framed. Would you like some coffee before you go?"

"No, I need to get going. Tell me how much I owe you, let's get the bird into your cage, and I'm going to run."

"But I'm taking you to the office."

"Ah, no, you might as well stop now you're home. I'll just grab a taxi outside."

Lucía tried to insist, but Roberta wouldn't budge.

"Tell me how much I owe you; then you can put the TV on and collapse on the sofa."

Lucía said she didn't owe her anything, that it had been like a vacation for her, but Roberta was adamant and threatened never to call again, so Lucía named her a cut price. She felt as though Roberta suddenly wanted to be rid of her. Her intuition told her something was wrong.

Though the bird was excited after all the to-ing

and fro-ing, it let Lucía take it out of the cage and transfer it to the other one.

"I'll get you a perch tomorrow, and not a second after," Lucía told the bird. "That way, you won't have to be cooped up in there all day long."

14

FOUR OR FIVE DAYS AFTER the trip to Toledo, she got a call from Ricardo, he of the stuffed-onion recipe and the out-of-date article. She agreed to pick him up outside the *El País* offices at midday.

It had been raining nonstop since the previous day. Large cold raindrops came down, driven against the car windows on all sides by high, swirling winds that had brought down four trees across the city. One had fallen on a bus, causing injuries of varying severity. This she heard on the 11:00 A.M. news bulletin. It also said there had been progress in the investigation into the death of Lucía's former boss, with the victim's cell phone having been found in the vicinity of the empty lot. The device was badly damaged, but the police were confident of being able to salvage at least some of the information on its internal memory. If so, they might be able to piece together the dead man's final movements.

The blood drained from Lucía's face as she started doing calculations. If they were able to establish where the asshole had commenced his journey to the empty lot, they could check all of the CCTV cameras along the way, and her taxi would be on the footage. She felt a stab of fear in the center of her belly, just above the tattoo, which kept her from inputting any more data into the algorithm. What with one thing and another, over the previous few days she had been having trouble constructing accurate flowcharts, and with imagining herself driving in Beijing, as well. It was beyond her to imagine that city in the rain. Where would the birds go in rain like this, and in cold like this?

Ricardo was there outside the newspaper's offices when she arrived, a black umbrella over his head like the one she had always imagined Braulio Botas carrying. She wondered why he wasn't sheltering inside, beyond the large expanse of ground-floor windows, when he could just as easily have kept an eye out from there.

Because he's only pretending to be coming out of the building, she thought.

The possibility that he was a policeman investigating the death of her asshole of a former boss immediately occurred to her. The moment she had abandoned the body came back: the complete darkness, the considerable distance she had been sure to put between herself and the bonfire zombies. They would have seen, perhaps, the silhouette of a car, maybe that of a woman getting out to off-load the body. . . . But from there to actually pinpoint-ing the vehicle, or indeed the identity of the driver in question . . . Yet there was still the question of the cell phone, presuming that was actually true and not a line by the police to try to flush out the culprit or culprits. In any case, he had been alive when she had dragged him out of the car, or she thought he had been. Where was the wrong in jet-tisoning a customer who was up to his eyeballs in goodness knows what manner of illicit drugs?

"Where to?" she asked when Ricardo, closing the umbrella, had settled in the backseat.

"To lunch," he said, shaking the rain off the lower parts of his trench coat.

"What do you mean, to lunch?"

"A bet's a bet. I lost, and I owe you lunch. We don't have to talk if you don't want to; you can ignore me, as though we aren't together. But gam-bling debts are sacred."

Lucía, soothed by this return to the everyday, smiled, turned the key in the ignition, and set off in the direction of the Chinese restaurant in Legazpi. She had no intention of asking any more questions. They caught each other's eyes in the rearview mir-ror a number of times, and both burst out laugh-ing. In one of these moments, she thought she saw Ricardo watching the meter.

"Hey, hey," she said, "I only turned it on when we got to Miguel Yuste."

"I didn't say anything."

"But you're looking at the meter like I'm taking you for a ride."

"That's not true. I don't know if you're like this with everybody, but you seem pretty paranoid with me."

"If your job consisted of having someone behind you constantly, I wonder what you'd be like."

"Well, there can't always be somebody in the taxi. Actually, isn't that exactly what you do want?"

"It's worse when there's no one, because then you're being watched by somebody who isn't there. The somebody who isn't there could be the most charming person in the world, or he could be a serial killer, depending on which side of the bed you got out on."

"And which side of the bed did you get out on today?"

"The gloomy side. All this wind and rain. But then I felt like something was going to happen, and look, it has."

"The something is me?"

"The something is you and me. The two of us together."

Although he tried to appear self-assured, she picked up on something unnatural in Ricardo, which registered as fleeting, panicked twinges in her body. Since the adventure with the cancer sufferer, she had not been to bed with anyone, and although she had been through longer periods in her life without sex—she knew perfectly well how to satisfy her own needs—on such an unpleasant day she felt the attraction of a few hours in somebody's arms, even if that somebody was an enemy.

"I'll drop you outside the restaurant, so you don't get wet," she said. "I'll go and park—let me have your umbrella. There's no point in both of us getting drenched."

"Okay," he said, "I feel like it should be the other way around, but I imagine I'm not allowed to drive a taxi without a license. I actually don't even have a driver's license."

"Well, that's that, then," she concluded, pulling up across from the restaurant. "But pay up for the fare now. I know myself, and I won't bother you for it after lunch."

"Cash or a card?" He laughed.

"Entirely up to you. By the way, I've still got the fifty-euro note you paid with last time."

"Why?"

"I'm planning to give it to someone in need."

Ricardo paid in cash.

COMING OUT OF THE PARKING LOT, Lucía opened the umbrella and made her way toward the restaurant, sticking close to the shop fronts and negotiating puddles as she went. When she was halfway there, the idea occurred to her of standing Ricardo up, just going straight back to the taxi. She didn't even know what his surname was—and his first name, that could just as well have been made up. She surmised a difference between the forces pushing her on and those telling her to go back, which was that the latter were purely rhetorical.

The restaurant did turn out to be very popular, and they would not have gotten a table had Ricardo not booked in advance. How far in advance? Lucía wondered.

"When did you book?" she asked as they sat down.

"The day before yesterday."

"So you're saying you made plans for me two days ago, and only bothered to let me know about them this morning."

"Don't start looking for things to get angry about. Who's to say I wasn't planning to come with somebody else, and that person couldn't make it at the last minute?"

"Now you're really making it all better."

"Okay. I thought that if I asked you two days in advance, that would mean two days for you to change your mind."

"And you didn't like the idea of that?"

"I didn't. Because I like you a lot, as you know."

Lucía had her hair up in the ballerina's bun that day, and she was wearing the same sweater and suede jacket she had worn the day of the encounter with the cancer sufferer. This, she thought, was why he had come to mind a moment before. What would have become of him? She decided she would give him a call at some point.

"What are you thinking about?"

"I was remembering the last man I went to bed with. I never found out his name or what line of work he was in. I picked him up outside the Palace Hotel and was supposed to take him to terminal four, and when *Turandot* started playing, he burst into tears. He had just been diagnosed with cancer."

"What kind?"

"I never found that out, either. He'd gotten the diagnosis here in Madrid, although he lived in Barcelona. We were on our way to the airport, but when we got to Colón, I turned around and we went back to the hotel. We spent the night together, and the next day I took him to the airport. I never heard from him again."

"How long ago was this?"

"A couple of months."

"He'll be dead, in that case."

"Why do you say that?"

"If he wasn't, he'd have called you again. Men, when something goes well for us, we keep repeating it—until it goes badly."

"Is that you talking, or the wine?" Lucía said incredulously.

"I've only had a couple of glasses. Now, is that lobster good or what?"

They had gotten to the main course, and the

verbal jousting that had been a constant since they'd first met continued unabated. Lucía wasn't drinking.

"I have to drive later on," she said.

"Come on, just one glass."

"It's my license on the line. But you were right, the lobster is out of this world. I think it's the first time I've ever had one."

"Tell me about life in a taxi."

"What about it?"

"Like, what do people talk about?"

"To me, or among themselves?"

"Either."

"In general, nothing at all."

"What do you mean, nothing at all?"

"Just like you and me right now. What are we talking about? Nothing."

"Hmm. There's something in that. Millions of people talking, the whole world over, and none of them saying anything. I'm going to write it down for one of my not-current articles."

Ricardo took out his cell phone and typed something into it at top speed, pressing the buttons with his thumbs.

"But the thing is to really imagine those millions of people," said Lucía. "They're in restaurants, in bars, in parks, in the street, in their bathrooms, living rooms, bedrooms, in the subway, riding the bus or train, in morgues—let's see, where else? In post offices, supermarkets, public bathrooms,

bathrooms in hotels, museums . . . Are you allowed to talk on the phone in museums?"

"I guess so. You're blowing my mind right now."

"Okay, in museums, too. So, all these millions of people with cell phones stuck to their ears, talking about nothing with another however many million people at the other end of the line. And not only in Spanish, like you and me now, but in hundreds or thousands of different languages. How many languages are there?"

"No idea."

"You're useless. The other day, since you ask, I picked a couple up at the airport. They were in their sixties, and I think they were Russian. They were going to the Ritz, and they talked the whole way in Russian, but from their faces, I could tell they were talking about nothing. Married couples, more than anyone, talk about nothing. Then, as well as everyone talking on the phone, you need to add people talking face-to-face, who generally don't talk about anything, either—even if they're talking Chinese, like everyone around us here."

When they looked around, they saw that they were the only Westerners in the restaurant. This felt uplifting to Lucía as, for a moment, it allowed her to reenter her Chinese fantasy.

"How do you know so much about people?" asked Ricardo.

"From observing them."

"And if you and I were to succeed in talking about something that wasn't nothing today?"

"It would be a truly heroic feat. Where shall we do it?"

"In your bed."

Lucía put the last piece of lobster in her mouth and held Ricardo's gaze for a long moment.

"Will you be getting up every two minutes to write down the things I say?"

"No, I promise."

"Fine, I'm going to take the chance, because you don't strike me as the dangerous type. By which I don't mean you aren't dangerous, because you are, in various ways, but all of them are counteracted by cowardice."

"You think I'm a coward?"

"In some people, it's a virtue."

"Again, how do you come to know so much about people?"

"Observation, like I say."

"Where to, then?"

"My place," said Lucía. "I prefer to tread on safe ground."

"That I find difficult to believe."

"There you go, reason for you to believe I'm a miracle."

Once Ricardo had paid the bill, Lucía said she would go and get the taxi on her own, taking his umbrella, and would be back to pick him up.

"No way," said Ricardo. "You'll only stand me

up; plus, you'll get my umbrella in the bargain. We'll go together, even if it means I get a bit more rained on than you."

And that was what they did, thereby initiating, with the rain as an excuse, their first physical contact.

"Promise me something," she said.

"Name it."

"That you won't turn cheap on me."

THEY ARRIVED AT Lucía's apartment half soaked and, both laughing, went into the living room, which was presided over by Calaf II's enormous cage.

"What's with the bird?" asked Ricardo.

"To pluck out your eyes if you misbehave."

Lucía went into the bathroom, freshened up, and came back out naked except for a dressing she had put over the tattoo, stuck down with see-through surgical tape. That was a present for Braulio Botas only, and she wasn't willing to let anyone see it before he did.

Ricardo was waiting by the bed in shirtsleeves, a little hesitant. He did not see the dressing because he did not dare look down that low.

"Shall I get you undressed, little one?" asked Lucía.

"Okay," he said.

She had barely so much as touched him when Ricardo went into a frenzy, one apparently pent up over weeks, or centuries.

"Whoa there," she suggested, though to no avail. He turned out to be the slightly complicated type, which in part was a disappointment to her and in part freed her of the fears she had begun to build up around him.

While they fucked, Ricardo on top, the rain pummeled the windowpanes as though it were falling horizontally.

"What's that?" he said when he reached down and his hand brushed against the dressing, which in his excitement he had failed to notice.

"A tattoo you're not allowed to see. Go on, don't stop."

AFTER A FEW ROUTINE POSITIONS, some proving more intense than others, but all a long way below Lucía's expectations, they fell asleep, Ricardo with his arms wrapped around her like he was riding behind her on a motorcycle. Lucía woke at close to 7:00 P.M. and found that the dressing had come off. It was completely dark outside. She got up and went to the bathroom to change the dressing. Then, without putting any clothes on, she went through the bedroom and into the living room, where she stood naked in front of

Calaf II. This was something she had been doing quite often, always in something of a fluster, as if in training for the moment when she would strip for Braulio Botas.

"I'm going to see if Bonehead is staying all night," she told the bird. "In this weather, I'd sleep with my arms around just about anything."

When she went into the bedroom, he opened his eyes. He looked startled.

"Are you looking at me like that because you don't know if you ought to like me or not?" asked Lucía.

"Ought to?"

"I'm pretend thin," she said, getting back into bed, "and a lot of men find it disconcerting."

"Tell me what you mean," he said, putting his arms around her.

"I'm fat, but I look thin. I've spent years moving among thin people without their realizing that I'm fat. Like a secret agent. Like a spy. When I'm driving the taxi, I look at fat people and say to them in my mind, I'm one of you, but even you don't know it. And then with thin people, I say, I'm not one of you, but I look like I am. I like spy movies because spies live in a world that isn't their own, and nobody realizes it."

"Now you are starting to scare me," he said.

"If you're staying the night, I'll make some spaghetti and tomato sauce."

"I'd love to, but I can't."

Looking at the clock, he jumped, or pretended to. She let it go.

"I'll call you," he said as he was leaving.

"No hurry," she said.

LUCÍA OPENED THE BIRDCAGE, and the bird flew out and came to land on the perch she had bought so that it could have a little more freedom. Sitting on the sofa, with her cell phone in her hand, she ran back through everything she and Ricardo had talked about, trying to unearth anything that would prove he was a policeman, but in the end she came up with nothing. She perceived a darkness in him, something murky she couldn't quite put her finger on, but he didn't seem to have anything to do with the case.

She then looked through her phone for the cancer sufferer's number, and when it appeared on the screen, she hesitated for a few moments before pressing the call icon. The ringtone sounded four times. A woman answered.

"Hello?"

"Good evening," she said, and, on the assumption that her number came up as that of a taxi driver, or a Madrid taxi driver, she decided to risk it. "I'm a taxi driver from Madrid, and the person whose number I've called was a client of mine. He used to call me for lifts when he came to Madrid, only it's been a while since I've heard from him. Are you his wife?"

She heard a sob at the other end of the line.

"I'm his widow."

"I can't tell you how sorry I am."

"He died yesterday; today's the vigil."

"I truly am sorry. He was the nicest, most polite person I've ever driven anywhere."

"Thank you."

"You're welcome."

Lucía tried to imagine the man inside the coffin. She saw his shroud as the same clothes she had taken off him in room 101 at the Palace Hotel. She imagined her business card pulsing in one of his pockets. She imagined the card in the ground, molding and decomposing in the damp and cold.

PART
TWO

15

THREE MONTHS HAD PASSED since Lucía had gotten the tattoo. Ninety days of an exceptionally cold winter, in the middle of which the Christmas holidays reared up like one more meteorological adversity. Nonetheless, Lucía was relieved to find it a less painful period in the taxi than going around on foot, especially when her earnings were double the usual amount. During those febrile days in which, come rain or shine, in the grip of a purely mechanical delirium, people shopped endlessly, the streets of Beijing came to predominate, fitting better to those of Madrid with every passing day. In a mysterious way, the junctions of the two cities, so geographically distant, so different in character, coincided on some deep, essential level, in the same way that twins separated at birth simultaneously experience the same highs and lows.

She used the map application on her cell phone as a GPS, most of the time with it switched to show the streets of Beijing. Curiously, none of her passengers realized, or if they did, they didn't say anything, until one day she picked up a Chinese man who worked at the embassy. Seeing the map, and seeing Lucía's makeup, the man laughed and asked what was going on, and she tried to make light of the situation, saying she was listening to *Turandot*.

"Just getting in the spirit," she said.

The man, who wasn't familiar with the Puccini opera, said he would be sure to get his hands on a copy.

She worked New Year's Eve, and had an average of two fares every hour for the duration of the night. At dawn, as she was driving home, she came across a teenage boy crying in the middle of her street, which was deserted. She drove past him, looked at him in the rearview mirror, and then reversed until she was alongside him. She rolled down the window.

"Hey, kid, what's going on?"

"Nothing," he said, turning to look at her.

"What do you mean, nothing? Then why are you crying?"

"No reason."

"Go on, come over here," she said consolingly.

The boy approached the window, wiping his runny nose on his jacket sleeve.

"What do you want?" he said.

"What do *you* want?" she replied.

"I don't know."

"Get in."

He did as he was told and sat in the passenger seat. Lucía started the engine after asking him to put his seat belt on.

They drove for a short while in silence, as the boy regained his composure. Lucía guessed him to be sixteen or seventeen.

"How old are you?" she asked.

"Eighteen."

"That means I can take advantage of you without being accused of perverting a minor."

The boy, who had stopped his crying by this point, blanched and looked over at Lucía with a mixture of panic and unalloyed desire.

"Don't worry," she said, putting her hand on his thigh for a brief moment. "I'm your fairy godmother."

The boy shifted in his seat, no doubt to accommodate his sudden erection.

"Disappointing New Year's Eve?" said Lucía.

"Right."

"They always are, but from time to time the miracle occurs."

"What miracle?"

"Me. Where do you live?"

The boy gave her an address in outlying Vallecas, which Lucía looked up on her map of Beijing. She then asked the boy to look at the map on her cell phone, which was mounted on the dashboard.

"What do you see?"

"I don't know. It says 'Beijing.'"

"That's because it's a map of Beijing."

"A map of Beijing?"

"You're seeing a map of Beijing because, due to a miracle, we have been transported there. Forget about shitty old Madrid, the place that made you cry. I'm a Chinese princess. Haven't you looked at my eyes? My name's Turandot."

"Right," said the boy flatly, still a little frightened.

"Say my name. Say, 'Hello, Turandot.'"

"Hello, Turandot."

They drove for another twenty minutes through the deserted city, neither of them saying a word. When they got to Vallecas, the boy started pointing out which streets to take.

"So many corners in Beijing," she said, handling the car easily in that grid of empty rain-washed streets.

"Right," he said, still fluctuating between excitement and fear.

Lucía turned her head, trying to meet his eyes.

"Are we there yet?" she asked.

"Yeah, that's my house, the one with the broken glass in the door."

Lucía found a space between the parked cars and pulled in. Then, putting an arm around the boy's shoulder, she pulled him close.

"You can bet none of your friends got to start the year like you."

She leaned in and kissed him on the mouth,

which tasted to her simply of mouth, nothing more. The boy let her kiss him for a few moments, but then his tongue came out in search of Lucía's, and they began to French-kiss, while their lips all but fused together. Straightaway, the boy's hands were on her breasts, and almost as soon as he started to knead them, he came in his underpants, whimpering like he was a newborn baby. And perhaps he was.

Lucía moved back from his embrace.

"Sorry," he said, bright red.

She smiled and stroked his head.

"The miracle is you," she said. "Go on, off to bed with you. And don't tell anyone about this; keep it just for you. Keep it just for you for the rest of your life, something that's nobody's but yours, incommunicable, completely yours. As though, rather than its having happened, you imagined it."

"Right," murmured the boy.

"Wait, come here a sec," she said when the boy had gotten out.

He came back over, and Lucía gave him the fifty-euro bill, which she had been keeping to give to someone more in need than she was.

She then waited until he was inside his house before driving away.

SHE HAD NOT HEARD from Roberta since the Toledo excursion, a short while before the holidays. She'd felt tempted to call her a few times, but shyness stopped her. She thought she had perhaps mistaken as friendship what for Roberta was nothing but a customer-vendor interaction. Ricardo had vanished as well, perhaps disappointed by their last encounter, or fearful of getting involved in something that would only bring problems in the long term.

In any case, he wasn't a policeman, or if he was, he had discarded her as a suspect.

As for Braulio Botas, he was still proving uncooperative, but nothing changed the fact that it was only a matter of time before he would appear, standing on a street corner, scanning the street for a taxi with his bird's eyes.

Every night when she got home, Lucía would undress in front of the mirror to check that the tattoo was still intact on her mons veneris, like one of those presents, the giving of which is delayed, meaning the wrapping needs changing from time to time. Here the wrapping was her underwear, which she updated over time, though the yearned-for encounter failed to materialize.

It was February—late February, in fact—and since the middle of January, the days had gradually been growing longer, and in the trees, even in those that were most damaged by the city's pollution, the first buds and flowers had started to appear, and the swifts were returning, and every day something was going to happen that never in fact happened. But she never lowered her guard, never went out unprepared for the possibility that it *would* happen. She always kept her mons completely shaved, so that the title of the aria was easily legible, and she always made sure to wear underwear befitting such a gift. She always applied her makeup with exactly the same care, and was discreet in perfuming herself. She always had the Puccini opera ready in the car stereo, like a bullet in the chamber.

16

IN HER SHORT TIME as a taxi driver, she had learned that some passengers are not passengers. They got in the car, yes, and they went from one place to another, but they weren't passengers in the strict sense. They were a mysterious, dubious kind of people, transmitting a vague unease and leaving a turbid atmosphere inside the vehicle, a mood that lingered almost no matter what Lucía did to try to clear it. There were different kinds of nonpassengers, though she would have been hard-pressed to identify exactly what distinguished them. In any case, the person sitting in the back at that moment was a nonpassenger. He had hailed her the very minute she had pulled out of her garage in the morning, as though he had been waiting for her. He was a man of about fifty, slightly scruffy, with a three- or four-day beard and a cheap jacket on.

"Good morning, sir," said Lucía. "Where to?"

"Julián González Segador," said the nonpassenger.

Lucía felt a jolt, but she didn't let on.

"To the Canillas Police Station, is that?" she asked.

"That's the one," said the man.

A policeman, she said to herself, possibly an on-duty one. She made a show of indifference while considering different ways of getting a conversation going. Or would it be more sensible not to?

"I can tell a policeman a mile off," she said eventually.

"And I can tell a firefighter a mile off, when he's dressed as a firefighter."

"But you're in civvies."

"In civvies, going to the Canillas Police Station . . ."

"Okay, yes," she conceded, "but it isn't because of where you're going so much as what you look like. You dress like Al Pacino in this one movie where he plays a policeman. I can't remember the title just now."

"I haven't seen it," said the man curtly.

"Well, it was a good one."

"And are you Chinese, or just pretending to be?"

"Ha. Pretending to be. Because of *Turandot*. Do you like opera?"

The man was no-nonsense. He gave the impression of looking for something.

"Have you always been a taxi driver?" he asked, rather than answering Lucía's question.

"No, I've only been doing it a few months."

"And what did you do before?"

"I was a systems analyst ... well, a programmer really. At an IT company that went bust."

"The one owned by that guy whose body they found in that lot?"

"So I'm told. Have they gotten to the bottom of that yet?"

"We're working on it."

"Well, good luck."

"When you're driving a taxi, you must pick up all sorts of different people."

This was starting to seem like an interrogation.

"Uh-huh."

"Hmm."

"I gave a lift to a home therapist yesterday. Know what that is?"

"No idea."

"Someone who heals houses."

"As in?"

"Someone who heals houses that are sick is the idea."

This was not true. She had heard about home therapists on a radio show in the small hours. There were people who did it as a job.

"And how do people know if a house is sick?" asked the policeman.

"Well, they know. Sometimes it's because there's sewage running under the house. Sometimes because something bad has happened there in the past, I don't know, in the kitchen, for instance, and the place remains impregnated with all the invisible pain."

"Right," said the nonpassenger. "And, going back to what we were talking about, did you know the deceased?"

"The asshole? At the company, that's what we used to call him. He used to start companies and shut them down like other people open and shut the fridge. But the answer is no; I saw him a couple of times in the hallway, going someplace. His office was on a different floor."

"And if one day he had gotten into your taxi, would you have called him an asshole?"

"I'm very professional; I treat everybody with the same respect."

The man paid in cash and got out of the taxi without saying good-bye.

LUCÍA DROVE A LITTLE WAY down the road, pulled over, and gave way to a full-blown panic attack that went on for three or four minutes. She then turned the taxi sign to red and started in the direction of Callao to go and find Roberta. She needed somebody to talk to, and nobody else came to mind. She had never been inside Roberta's office, but she thought she would just walk in and ask her to go for breakfast, inventing some cause for celebration on the way. She would not tell her what had happened, of course, but by her estimation, the mere fact of seeing Roberta would help alleviate her anxiety.

As she was driving along Gran Vía, passing the Chicote cocktail bar, she saw from behind two people who looked familiar. They were going into Hotel de las Letras. One of the backs she recognized as belonging to Roberta. The other to Ricardo. And they were together, arm in arm. Lucía instinctively hung a right, turning into the Vázquez de Mella parking lot. When she came back out onto the street, she could hardly breathe.

Thinking to herself that she must have been hallucinating, she crossed the street but walked straight into a blind lottery ticket vendor on the pedestrian crossing, knocking him to the ground. She stopped to help him back up.

"I shit on your soul," the blind man said to her.

As she cautiously approached the café window, she thought about the soul as being like a soap bubble filled with smoke. She had not been hallucinating. There they were, Ricardo and Roberta, sitting at a table, laughing and chatting happily away.

What was happening to reality?

This was not happening in Beijing, or in Madrid, or in any other place that might be pointed to on a map, unless it were an intangible map, because it was happening in a moral dimension of existence, of her own existence. She tried to start constructing an algorithm, because algorithms were something she always found calming, but what was the input data with which to begin this particular flowchart?

Chart of vaginal flows, she remembered.

Something's going to happen inside that which is already happening, she said to herself. And it did, because at that moment she saw Braulio Botas walk into the café, through the door on the Gran Vía side, and join Ricardo and Roberta at their table. He was dressed almost for summer, in jeans and a light brown leather jacket and matching shoes. Under the jacket was a black T-shirt with a design on it that Lucía could not quite make out from where she was. The waiter went over to the group, wrote down their order, and went away again. A woman passed Lucía, holding a girl by the hand. The girl was crying. The woman said she couldn't have everything. Then a man stopped to light a cigarette, the first puff of which, having been drawn down into his lungs and exhaled, wafted past Lucía's nose.

Camels, she said to herself.

A couple hurtled past, having an argument. The woman was saying, "I always knew you poked holes in the condoms."

The waiter returned shortly with three steaming cups, coffee or tea. Roberta, Braulio, and Ricardo toasted one another with them, then each took a sip before setting the cups down and going on with their apparently gleeful conversation.

For fear of being discovered, and once she had made absolutely sure that she was not deceived as to the trio's identity, Lucía turned and headed back in the direction of the parking lot. She went to cross at the same pedestrian crossing where she had crashed into the blind man. It was while waiting for the light to turn green that she felt the first transformations beginning to take place in her body; it seemed that her legs, under her jeans, had mutated into the legs of a bird. She crossed the street, moving somewhat spasmodically, like a bird. Then her mouth began to elongate outward from the center, and to harden, until it became a beak. An invisible beak, like the ghost limbs experienced by amputees; in fact, though it was certainly there, when she lifted her hands to her face, she was unable to feel it. She glanced around to see if anyone was noticing what was happening to her, and people did seem to be giving her a wide berth, though with no excessive show of alarm. She saw the sign for a pharmacy, read it with one eye, then the other, and went on in the direction of the parking lot with her bird legs hidden beneath her jeans.

Could she drive?

Once she was inside the taxi, she took her shoes off to see if her feet were those of a woman or a bird, and, to look at, they were a woman's, though she felt like she was looking at them with bird's eyes. She had a go at putting her foot down on the brake and the accelerator, and found that, though not entirely straightforward, it was at least doable. But she proceeded with utmost caution as she started the engine, and succeeded in making it all the way home without incident.

When she got to the apartment, she took her clothes off and stood in front of the mirror, which reflected back the image of a woman, though her inner perception was that of a bird. This bird had a curved, very hard beak, capable of ripping out a man's stomach wall and eviscerating him. She saw herself doing this to Braulio Botas. Evisceration was in her thoughts because, reading up on the Internet about birds recently, she had come across an article about Prometheus, the Greek hero condemned to having his liver eternally pecked at by an eagle; every day, a new liver would regenerate to be pecked anew. She imagined Braulio Botas chained to her bed, and her rummaging around for his guts with her beak while *Turandot* played on the stereo.

"Why the punishment?" Calaf II suddenly asked. Lucía could understand him perfectly.

"What punishment?" asked Lucía.

"Prometheus's."

"He stole fire from the gods, I think."

She could not tell whether she and the bird were talking inside their minds, or making actual sounds, but what was for certain was that they could understand each other perfectly well.

"You're worn-out," the bird said to her from its perch.

"Yes," she said, "I need to sleep."

"Leave the living room window open and go and get into bed."

Lucía did as the bird told her, and was soon between the sheets, lying on her side in the fetal position so as not to damage her wings. Before her eyes fell shut, she did some calculations.

Input data, she said to herself: Roberta, Ricardo, and Braulio Botas were friends. Roberta and Ricardo, possibly more than that. Roberta had told them about meeting a very flamboyant female taxi driver who was enamored of the actor, and who went around Madrid made up to look like a Chinese person, while listening to *Turandot* on repeat.

"A madwoman," she would have finished by saying.

Then she had given them both Lucía's number, which up until now only Ricardo had used, so they could have a chance to enjoy her nonsense for themselves. Botas still had not shown himself, and there was no way of knowing if he ever would. Perhaps when she saw them in the café at Hotel de las Letras, they were laughing about her and encouraging the actor to look her up, telling him it would be worth his while.

"Seriously," she imagined them saying, "she's not to be missed."

All of which was to say, Lucía had fallen into a snare set by people better educated than she, and she did not know how to get out of it. She saw herself flapping her wings and kicking her legs inside an invisible net, the knots of which damaged her plumage. Thus, the bird part of her writhing about, and the human part of her beset by a fever that surely had her temperature soaring beyond the limits of normal thermometers, she fell into a stupor that gave way to dreams full of insubstantial tunnels as dark as the very deepest galleries of the mind.

Hours later, or perhaps it was days or centuries—she could not have said—she felt something moving about between her lips and, still feverish, opened her eyes, to find Calaf II pushing some sort of foodstuff into her mouth.

"Tastes green," she murmured.

"Eat it and go back to sleep," Calaf II ordered.

And she did. She slept a dreamless sleep, as the caterpillar must as it turns into a butterfly. Calaf II woke her from time to time to feed her a worm or some other gobbet, possibly chunks of bread previously softened for her in the bird's own saliva.

While she slept, and while the fever veered from scorching highs to teeth-chattering lows, the metamorphosis ran its course. So that one day, in the second week of March, she woke in a puddle of cold sweat and emerged from between the sheets having assumed the form of a very powerful eagle. Her visible body remained that of a woman, but her ghost body was a bird's. And both were completely compatible. She did find that she had to recalculate the distances between herself and things around her in physical space, because she at times tried to reach out for something tangible with her ghost body, or vice versa, producing corporeal mismatches that, out in the wider world, could prove catastrophic. She therefore stayed inside the apartment a few days longer, practicing movements under the watchful gaze of Calaf II, to his approval or otherwise—because his problem, as he explained to Lucía, was the reverse: His visible body was that of a bird, his ghost body a man's.

"Did the two of us copulate while I was asleep?" Lucía asked.

"Maybe." He cackled.

Once she had formed an understanding of the possibilities and limitations of the two bodies, it became possible to walk on her human legs and, using her eagle wings, to take to the air. Every time she bumped her head on the apartment ceiling, she laughed and floated gently back to earth.

Before going out into the world again, she went through the missed calls and messages on her cell phone to see if there was anything from Roberta or Ricardo. As she had expected, they'd had their fun and moved on.

17

SHE RETURNED TO DRIVING the taxi without the Chinese makeup on, so that when Braulio Botas appeared on a street corner looking for a taxi, he would not immediately recognize her as the madwoman about which the others had undoubtedly told him. And although they had been neighbors, Lucía thought their encounter over the bogus leak would not, as it had for her, have left the slightest mark on him. On the other hand, her conversion into a bird woman had also brought profound changes in her physical constitution. She was thin now, a genuinely thin person, and her face had become as long and thin as her mother's on her deathbed, if not more so. She had also cut her hair short and now brushed it back and up in a way reminiscent of an eagle's plume. She was occasionally put in mind of her asshole ex-boss. There had been no contact from the police, but in any case, from her newly acquired bird's-eye view, it seemed a matter of little importance, something that would disappear from her head as quickly as it had appeared.

She dressed normally, too, since her vigor no longer emanated from her outer trappings, but from the bird into which she had mutated. The organs of the woman and the bird interwove in such a way that at points she would simply sit back and let the creature take control of both bodies. At this particular moment, for instance, while her human feet worked the pedals in the car and her five-fingered hands gripped the steering wheel, the head on her shoulders was that of an eagle, with that beautiful plume, the wary eyes, and steely beak. The passenger in the seat behind her didn't notice a thing because the bird body was invisible, intangible, though at the same time as undeniable as the wind, which, though invisible to the eye and impossible to physically get hold of, knocks down trees all the same.

She had just picked the man up at Reina Victoria, near the old Red Cross building, and after asking to be taken to Moncloa, he had taken out his cell phone and proceeded to argue (with his wife, Lucía deduced) about a hole that had appeared in the parquet of their living room floor.

"A hole in the parquet?" he asked.

Lucía couldn't make out the woman's answer, though her voice came through in microscopic noises, bitty and shrill, as though broken glass were being ground under the toe of somebody's boot.

"The building doesn't have mice," the man

said. "In any case, there's nothing I can do about it from Barcelona."

When he hung up, he gave Lucía an exculpatory smile.

"Sorry," he said, "I'm not crazy. My wife just thinks I'm in Barcelona."

"Not to worry, I'm in Beijing. Look at the GPS."

The passenger leaned forward and looked. Lucía felt as though she would be able to swivel her head around, faster than the speed of light, and use her beak to tear a strip from his cheek.

"Beijing?" said the man. "What's that about?"

"What's that about Barcelona?" replied Lucía.

The man smiled in a somewhat leering manner.

"Just my bit on the side."

"Ah," she said.

Perhaps he thought he could seduce the taxi driver. In fact, he had started eyeing her up before but was afraid to go on doing so after their eyes met in the rearview mirror, and he found himself confronted with the unexpected animal gleam therein. It was the first time Lucía had tested out the effect of her bird gaze on a human specimen. Smiling inwardly with her human mouth, she half-turned to face him with her eagle head.

"You find me slightly frightening, don't you?"

"Frightening? No." He was lying. "Why?"

"That's for you to say. I thought you were going into your shell."

Lucía thought she sensed the man getting an

erection, provoked by a panic of a sexual order, and this, in turn, awakened her bird's genitalia, which coexisted in her insides in the same way the maps of Madrid and Beijing coexisted in the GPS, or Madrid and Barcelona inside this man's head.

"Have you got an erection?" she asked.

"What?"

"Don't worry about it. The world is full of erections."

The man, who had traveled to Barcelona for a night on the town without any need of leaving Madrid, was clearly starting to hanker for the domestic complications related to the hole in the living room parquet, and he took out his cell phone and called his wife. He said he'd decided to come home early, today in fact, because the sale had already gone through and he felt like sleeping in his own bed.

He paid in cash. A lot of people got rid of undeclared income by paying in cash.

Lucía started the engine. She was slightly aroused, and so she drove to the Moncloa University campus, looking for a quiet street, which, approaching the Forensics Institute, she found. She parked, put *Turandot* on, skipped forward to "Nessun dorma," and reclined her seat. Today she was wearing an old skirt instead of her jeans, which were too big on her now. She hitched the skirt up, pulled the gauzy fabric of her panties aside with her left hand, and guided her right to the focal point of her ardor. She had been playing with herself for only a few seconds when she perceived that the organs she was caressing were not those of her human self, but those of the bird, and it was then the bird that turned out to be the recipient of the savage orgasm that soon cascaded through her; it beat its wings in desperation and opened its steely beak as wide as it could as a cry rose from deep in its guts, breaking the silence like a silk cloth being torn in the middle of the night, just as the aria reached its conclusion: "All'alba vincerò! Vincerò! Vincerò!"

Arriving back in the center of the city, as the aria went on playing on the stereo as well as inside her mind, she saw herself turning circles over the Beijing square, looking down on the heads of the failed suitors on their spikes.

18

THAT DAY IN EARLY APRIL, after taking a passenger to the Puerta de Toledo, she turned the radio on to listen to the 11:00 A.M. news, but the murder of her ex-boss did not feature. At the end of the bulletin came the arts and culture section, and there was mention of a forthcoming play with Braulio Botas as the leading man, followed by an interview with Botas himself.

"Is the play called *What I Know of Myself* because it reveals little-known aspects of your own life?"

"Well," said the actor, "given that I came up with the idea for the play, and I wrote it, it does contain some elements of autobiography. That's always the way. But it's important not to be too literal here. That which is autobiographical often hides behind the very polar opposite of things that happen in one's own life."

"But the title suggests there are things about yourself that you don't know."

"Of course. We're generally very ignorant when it comes to ourselves. Therefore, the things *not* mentioned in the play are just as important as those that are. It's Hemingway's iceberg theory. He said that ninety percent of a story ought to remain hidden, and that's what keeps the ten percent afloat."

"It's a long time since you've done any acting. Why?"

"In part because my teaching has been too all-consuming—though that isn't to say I don't enjoy it. Teaching means actors can experiment, and helps us acquire a deeper knowledge of what we do."

The interviewer, after saying that the premiere was the following Thursday in the Teatro Español, said "Good-bye" and "Break a leg" to the actor.

Lucía found somewhere to pull over, took out her cell phone, and went on the website for the Teatro Español, finding that only four or five seats had sold for Botas's play. Perhaps the tickets had only just gone on sale. She selected an aisle seat in the front row, entered her credit card details, and paid for the ticket before setting off in the taxi once more. Perhaps she would not go to the play after all—she had to think it through—but the mere possibility of doing so produced a wholesome feeling of euphoria in her.

She worked late that evening; there were a lot of people out and she was ferrying passengers around almost constantly. When she got home, Calaf II was asleep on his perch.

Evening, said Lucía inside her mind.

The bird did not answer, but it did lift its head and fly the short distance to the cage before shutting the door behind itself with its beak.

Lucía took an uncooked steak out of the fridge and proceeded to tear chunks from it with her teeth while walking around the apartment. Before getting into bed, she went on the Teatro Español website and checked that her reservation had gone through. Since the radio interview, another dozen or so tickets had sold. That wasn't many, she thought.

19

THE DAY OF THE PREMIERE of *What I Know of Myself,* she arrived at the theater a few hours early and walked the surrounding streets like a secret agent scouting out the site of a clandestine meeting in advance. The weather was good, and all the bar terraces were full; spring was a welcome change after the bitter, sodden winter. Lucía, still very slim, was dressed in a long patterned skirt, a black tank top, and sneakers. She had no makeup on. Every seven or eight paces, with a flap of her ghost eagle wings, she gave a small skip; otherwise, the eagle was idle inside her. She could tell that the bird did not really feel like doing this, so Lucía let it be and went into the theater bar, which was overflowing with people there for the premiere, among them some well-known TV personalities. She took a seat at the end of the bar and ordered a bottle of water.

Half an hour before the show was due to start, Roberta and Ricardo entered the bar—chatting animatedly, very much together—immediately to be accosted by lots of people they appeared to know. Endless kisses and handshakes ensued as they made their way to the bar; they ended up a few seats away from where Lucía was sitting, though they didn't notice her, despite her glaring at them. They ordered two vodka tonics.

"And some chips," added Roberta. "I'm starving."

"You're nervous," said Ricardo.

The doors opened fifteen minutes before the start, and Lucía was one of the first to go and find her seat. She was slightly disappointed by the size of the theater, but she guessed it was normal on the "alternative circuits" in which, as Roberta had told her, Braulio Botas plied his trade. Nor was there a theater curtain, meaning that the single prop, a Madrid taxi right in the middle of the stage, was on full view. She observed everything—herself included—with a kind of Sunday-afternoon calm, which even she found a little perturbing.

The moment arrived, the houselights went down, the stage lights gradually came up, and, to everyone's surprise, one of the taxi doors opened and out stepped Braulio Botas. He was wearing a pair of plain black jeans and a matching T-shirt. He was, as Lucía remembered, an out-and-out bird man: thin, delicate, with that messy shock of very white hair—like a bird that had just flown out the other side of a storm. It sent a chill down Lucía to see him move to the front of the stage and stop at the edge. He then bowed his head, whether in reverence or in concentration, before looking out into the audience, putting those sitting there under the hypnotic spell of his bird gaze. For several seconds, he said nothing, producing an uncomfortable sense of paralysis in the auditorium; this succeeded in cranking up the tension. Everybody, in those moments, sat rooted; nobody so much as dared to clear his or her throat. He then proceeded to walk from one end of the stage to the other with his long heron- or flamingolike stride before finally addressing the spectators in a confiding tone.

"Here you have me: a pretend-thin person."

There was some muffled laughter here and there, while the eagle asleep inside Lucía began to flap its wings in agitation.

"Pretend thinness," he continued, "isn't to be confused with hidden obesity. Hidden obesity is a clinical diagnosis, while pretend thinness is a metaphysical concept."

Then, with the actor set to continue his soliloquy, a woman appeared on the side of the stage, having apparently walked that way by accident.

"Sorry," she said, "I was trying to find my seat and . . ."

The public, still not knowing whether this was scripted or not, burst into laughter, this time in unison. The woman stood frozen, clutching a large, rather cheap-looking tote bag. She looked more like she had stepped out to buy groceries than to go to the theater.

"Well, since you're here," said Botas, beckoning her to join him at center stage.

And then, solemnly addressing the audience, he said, "This is one of those curious moments in which life seeps into fiction. Here," he said, pointing to the woman, "you have life. And addressing you now is fiction. Put it another way: You have before you a person and a character, all for the price of a single ticket."

The audience's immobility was matched only by its hushed silence. Botas managed the silences with stunning aplomb. He was looking at the woman now, as though expecting an answer. But she, gripped by panic, backed away, without succeeding in actually getting off the stage.

"Help us clear something up, would you?" said Botas. "What does life have to say to fiction?"

It took the woman a moment or two to react. Finally, falteringly, she said, "If it's all the same to you, I'd rather tell you what fiction would say to life."

"Go for it."

"It would say, 'Where are you going in such a hurry?'"

The single organism comprised of the audience members burst into peals of laughter. Botas looked less than pleased—as though the woman were stealing his thunder.

"Okay, off you go," he said, pushing her back in

the direction of the seats. "You go back to life, leave fiction to the experts."

While the woman went and took a seat, the lights dimmed and Botas went back to his initial position, as though, the interruption dealt with, he was about to start over. Thus he got into the taxi again, and out of it again, repeating the very same steps he had at the beginning.

"Before being a taxi driver," he said, "I worked as a programmer. When reality goes wrong, I just do a restart."

This was met with more laughter, and Botas waited patiently, allowing it to spread infectiously from seat to seat.

"When fiction goes wrong, I also do a restart," he continued. "But fear not, we've got plenty of time to discuss the relationship between life and fiction, between character and *the* character. Now let's go back to the start. I was telling you that I was a pretend-thin person."

The stage lights then came fully up once more, while the opening strains of *Turandot* started to play. Botas reacted as though surprised.

"Hear that?" he said. "That music isn't part of this play; it's from the show that's going on in the main theater, next door, but it's filtering through like something produced by a moment that is separated from our own by a dimensional wall. I find it unsettling because, though I detest opera, anytime

I hear it from the other side of a wall, it succeeds in making me very emotional."

The audience, completely rapt, unsure what was meant to be part of the show and what was not, laughed once more, while the eagle stretched out inside Lucía.

From there on, though in a different order, she heard a version of everything she had told Roberta and Ricardo. Botas, poised and articulate, described the day when, having lost his job as a programmer, he went home and heard "Nessun dorma" coming through the bathroom vent from the apartment below.

"I sat down on the bidet and cried," he said. "I had just turned the age my mother was when she died."

Next he talked about his mother's having been a bird woman, and recounted the events of his tenth birthday, seeing her going out to pee in the garden and a blackbird flying down and crashing into her head. And how a sort of soap bubble, full of smoke, had emerged from the bird's beak and entered his mother's body through her mouth.

He talked about his decision to go and meet this neighbor who kept playing Puccini on repeat, and described him and Lucía meeting, though with him in Lucía's role. This downstairs neighbor, he said, had subsequently vanished, and he had spent the following months driving around

Madrid or Beijing—he wasn't sure which—waiting for the woman to appear and step into his taxi.

While telling his own story—Lucía's story—Botas also narrated the story of *Turandot*, cleverly interweaving the two event-filled plots. He detailed the fantasy of driving around Beijing, instead of Madrid, and the mysterious convergence of the respective cities' maps in his mind. He also gave a description of the square in Beijing where Turandot's palace was situated, and spoke about the impaled heads of the suitors decorating it, the birds descending to help themselves to an eyelid or an eyeball. And every one of the story elements that emerged from his mouth was joined to the previous and then to the following in such way that it kept the audience fully absorbed, except for in the moments when laughter broke out, which was often, since it was nothing if not a comically naïve character being presented. Meanwhile, the eagle had awakened fully and adopted a sedentary posture, its claws gripping the arms of Lucía's seat and its head thrust in front of Lucía's, as though Lucía had withdrawn inside the creature, and it was from there that she heard the braying audience, egged on by the actor with all his knowing expressions of perplexity.

Nothing was missing from the script, neither Lucía's challenging childhood nor the memory of her bird mother, her love for the actor nor her existential struggles; even the dead cancer sufferer got a mention. The piece ended with Botas coming to the front of the stage and confessing that he had hired the theater in the hope that his actress would come to the show. He then peered out into the crowd, looking at the audience members almost one at a time, trying to pick her out. In the end, finding her not there, he withdrew to the rear of the stage while "Nessun dorma" rang out at full volume. And so nothing went unprofaned. The lights dimmed as the actor climbed back into the taxi, and the engine roared as he turned the key in the ignition. The audience, after a few moments of mournful quiet, erupted into clapping, along with cries of "Bravo!" everyone exhorting the actor to get out and acknowledge the applause. The lights went back up and Braulio Botas emerged, exultant. He looked around the auditorium, thanking and blowing kisses to people he knew, of which there were presumably quite a few, since it was the premiere. Then his eyes met Lucía's, but he must have seen the eagle instead of the woman, because the color drained from his face and he seemed almost to faint—which the audience took to be part of the show, redoubling their cheers and applause as the actor steadied himself and, avoiding looking in Lucía's direction again, invited first the actress who had played the lost woman and then the writer-director to join him onstage. Lucía and the eagle then saw Ricardo appear onstage. And, indeed, Ricardo was not called Ricardo, but, as it said in the program, Santiago Cáceres, the award-winning writer-director.

Lucía left the theater walking on the eagle's legs, her own having turned to paper. She had walked in as a real-life person and was now coming out of it as a comic, or at best tragicomic, character. The eagle walked away down calle Prado, as far as the taxi stand outside the Palace Hotel, getting into the first waiting taxi, given that she would have been quite unable to drive.

"Where to?" said the man driving.

Lucía came up from the depths of the bird to give the man her address before returning to them, and stayed there until they got to where they were going.

20

AFTER A NUMBER OF DAYS recovering, with Calaf II once more taking care of her, Lucía returned to the outside world to play the role she had been assigned. She was even thinner than before, but at the same time more vigilant of the dangers around her, more agile and maneuverable. She drove the taxi with a certain efficiency, and spoke to the passengers using conversational codes obtained from certain painstakingly wrought algorithms. It was a mercifully warm April, and Lucía kept the apartment windows open, meaning Calaf II could come and go as he pleased. She sometimes returned at night and found the bird not there, but she had only to turn on the lights for it to reappear soon, almost always bearing some gift or other in its beak: a shard of glass, a steel washer, an empty blister pack, an old and very worn-out toothbrush ... Shiny little knickknacks that Lucía put together in a cardboard box like a stash of booty that, from a place of fiction, she and the bird had succeeded in snatching from reality.

That Monday began with rain. Going to the window, with her keen eagle sense of smell, Lucía picked up on the unmistakable scent of spring storms.

Something's going to happen.

She set out in the taxi as the heavens opened. The frenetic windshield wipers did little to help the visibility. The massive raindrops, with the occasional hailstone thrown in, drummed on the bodywork of the taxi, somewhat akin to background music in a movie during the buildup to a crime. At the first set of traffic lights she came to, she picked up a man who emerged from a doorway at a run, a plastic folder over his head as an umbrella.

"Now that's what I call luck," he said as he settled in his seat.

Lucía courteously listened as he gave her the address, turned the meter on, and then put "Nessun dorma" on the stereo at full volume. Her spirit felt comforted by the storm, and she started to sing in duet with Pavarotti, not the slightest bit interested in what the passenger, looking on with a condescending smile, thought of her.

"These spring storms," he said, "generate negatively charged ions, which, in turn, make people euphoric."

"It must be that," she said before he could continue.

And immediately afterward, as written in the stars, and as the "Vincerò" of the final verse came in, there, some fifty meters along from the corner of calle Serrano and Juan Bravo, was the silhouette of Braulio Botas, wrapped in a trench coat that was too big for him and holding a black umbrella over his head evocative of a giant bird's wings. He was jerking his head from side to side, trying to spot the green light of an unoccupied taxi.

Lucía turned the stereo off, came to a screeching halt, and, turning to the passenger, ordered him to get out.

"What?" said the man, gesturing to the weather in which she was proposing to leave him.

Lucía's eyes were momentarily replaced by those of the eagle, and they gave the man a withering look while she repeated herself—"I said, get out"—with a kind of cawing noise, because her throat was also the eagle's now. The terrified man obeyed immediately. She started the taxi and drove up to where Botas was standing. He closed his umbrella and, puffing out his cheeks, got in.

"What a day!" he said, laying the umbrella in the footwell to avoid getting the seats wet.

"It's beautiful!" said Lucía. "The atmosphere is charged with negative ions, and they make you euphoric."

"Must be negative," he said. "The Teatro Español, please, on Plaza Santa Ana."

"Have you got a rehearsal?"

"Pardon?"

"Sorry, but I recognize you. You're Braulio Botas, the actor. I saw your play."

"Ah!" he said, clearly flattered. "And did you like it?"

"Loved it. I don't go to the theater much, but a colleague told me the main character was a taxi driver and, naturally, I was interested. You're brilliant."

"Well, thank you very much."

"And all the crazy stuff in your script, some of it funny, some of it so deep . . . I often find myself thinking things like that. You get a lot of time to think when you drive a taxi. Between all the different people you see, the conversations you overhear, and the hours when you're alone, trying to spot your next fare, some days you go to bed having thought more about things than a whole army of philosophers."

"Really?"

"Really. And that's the great thing about your character, because he skips from one idea to another like a bird hopping around all over the place. I'm convinced that the writer—what was his name?"

"Santiago Cáceres."

"That was it, Cáceres. I'm convinced he must have done proper, on-the-ground research to have written all of that. He hits the nail on the head, take it from me."

"I suppose so," said Botas cautiously.

"And you? Did you do any research?"

"Well, not as much as he did. When you're handed a script that works really well, all the guidance you need is right there. I'm not one of these actors who needs to spend months in an asylum to play a madman."

"Well, a bit of time in the taxi with me wouldn't go amiss; then you could see what this world is really like. It'd be sure to improve your performance. . . ."

Lucía's suggestive lilt was not lost on the actor, who began to observe her calculatingly.

"Are you in a hurry?" she said. "Because you can already see what the traffic's like."

"Actually, no. The show isn't on today—Monday's our rest day. I was going to the theater to work on a couple of scenes with the director, but it isn't much of a day to be out and about. If I didn't know it was morning, I'd swear the sun was going down."

"Well, just stay in the taxi, then. It's like being at home."

Braulio Botas's eyes gave a doubtful flicker. He then looked at Lucía in the rearview mirror, a frank, unguarded look that seemed to say, Yes or no? She smiled and winked.

"If you really want to know what it's like to be a taxi driver, I could show you my apartment."

"You live alone?" he said, moving to the informal *tú* address.

"Yes. Too alone, sometimes. Not that I'd have it any other way, I'm no good in relationships, but on rainy days like today, I certainly wouldn't mind having someone next to me to watch a movie with. . . ."

Botas smiled, obviously pleased. He then took out his cell phone and, without another thought, canceled his meeting.

"In that case, do with me as you will."

Lucía rapidly began to think about the problem of Botas's having lived in the very same building before, and his likely questions when they arrived.

"I'll just see where I can turn around," she said. "I live on the corner of Canillas and Cartagena. I just recently rented an apartment from a colleague."

The actor seemed perturbed by this, and Lucía added, "She sold her license because she was going abroad."

"Oh?" he said.

"To Mallorca, I think."

"Was that long ago?"

"No, just a few weeks."

The actor relaxed.

"It so happens," he said, "I lived at that very same address at one point. So your colleague and I must have been neighbors."

"I guess so!" she said.

Lucía turned right off Colón onto the Paseo de la Castellana, going in the direction of María de

Molina. The rain had abated somewhat, and the windshield wipers would pause every now and then for a few moments. She could feel, with her eagle senses, the actor's state of arousal, which was met and equaled deep in Lucía's human belly. In his excitement, Botas went on talking.

"In fact," he said, "I think I met her."

"Who?"

"Your colleague. She lived on the fourth floor, and I lived on the third floor. She came down to my apartment one day because there had been a leak in her kitchen. But I moved out pretty much straight after that, and we didn't see each other again."

"In *What I Know of Myself,* it has it the other way around; it's the taxi driver who goes down to her apartment when she's listening to *Turandot,* right?"

"Exactly. And something you couldn't otherwise know: Cáceres, the writer, was inspired by that meeting."

"Well, I never."

"And were you very friendly with this colleague of yours?"

"No, not at all. I heard about her renting the apartment on the radio. It all happened very quickly. There was some hurry for her to leave. I didn't even meet her, because she left it all in the hands of an agent and I signed the contract with him. We spoke on the phone, and she asked if I could look after her bird, which she wasn't allowed to take yet. The apartment was at a really good price, so I said yes. Now I've developed a soft spot for the bird. The way it goes, I guess."

"Well, she must have been quite a character; through a series of coincidences, the writer had quite a few dealings with her."

"Sure, but I couldn't really say. You get all sorts in this job; as a sector, it's forever changing. Every time a company shuts down, somebody, with the severance pay, buys themself a taxi license."

"Like your colleague, who was a programmer before she started driving taxis."

"And like the character in the play!"

"Right."

Lucía, though she knew the possibility was remote, had hoped that Botas knew nothing about Roberta's and so-called Ricardo's plotting, and now she tried to brush over the pain of his words with a seductive smile in the rearview mirror.

It was a twenty-minute drive to María de Molina, which she took in the direction of avenida de América, from which she turned onto Cartagena. In the downpour, the traffic had grown worse; the roads were like a great vegetable soup, clotted with vehicles. Thanks to the eagle's razor-sharp faculties, combined with her female organs, Lucía noticed the sexual temperature rising inside the bubble of the car.

"Easy, tiger," she said, giving Botas a wink. "We'll be there any minute."

"You just keep your eyes on the road. If we crashed, we wouldn't get to have our fun."

"It must be very easy for actors to have adventures like this, right?" said Lucía, beginning to sense a disappointing cheapness in Botas.

"For taxi drivers as well, I imagine."

"Well, it isn't just any old passenger I go to bed with. Put it down to the negative ions from the storm, and how much I enjoyed the play. It's like I'm giving you something back for what you've given me."

"I never *gave* you anything; I imagine you paid for your ticket."

"And you're going to pay for the ride, so don't go getting any ideas!"

They both laughed.

"Finally," said Lucía as they pulled into the garage.

Once they were going up in the elevator, Botas brushed her lips with his, just as he had done the first time they met. It must have been his method. His breath smelled familiar to her—she would not have forgotten it in a thousand years—and she exhaled a little of her own, which the actor savored like a perfume.

"Mmm . . ." he said.

When they went into the apartment, Botas

raised an eyebrow at the sight of Calaf II on his perch. Lucía spoke before he had a chance to.

"This is the bird I inherited, temporarily, from the landlady. It's very sociable."

The actor went over to stroke Calaf II's head, receiving a peck on the hand for his troubles.

"Son of a—"

"He's seen into your soul," joked Lucía. "He's got a nose for detecting bad people."

She went through into the bedroom, with Botas following behind, and started to undress. She took off everything except for her panties.

"No preamble, then?" he said, taking off the trench coat.

"I prefer the postamble," she replied, smiling.

"You're starting to frighten me a little," said Botas, stripping off. "I don't know if I'm going to be up to it."

"Don't you worry, I'll lend a hand."

When Botas was down to his undershorts, Lucía went over and pulled them down.

"What a letdown!" she said. "No 'Nessun dorma' tattoo on your pubis like your character in the play has!"

"Of course not, babe, that was fiction; this is reality. That's what *What I Know of Myself* is partly about: people who confuse the one with the other."

"Well, what would happen if I did? Here, down you get. . . ."

The actor bent down, at first with a disbelieving smile, until, as she lowered her panties to reveal the tattoo, he laid eyes on it. But his arousal won out over his surprise, meaning he offered no resistance when she took him by the hair and pulled his head close to her vagina; he commenced kissing her there, and then to licking up her wetness. And as he began to lose himself in the task, his tongue diving into the eagle's intimate folds and creases—mistaken by him for Lucía's folds and creases—he received a blow to the left side of his temple, and toppled onto his side, unconscious.

Lucía gave a pained grimace. She had hit him with her own fist, but impelled by the eagle's fierce energy. Although, she supposed, it would take him some time to come around, she hurried into the kitchen for a roll of tape to fasten his hands to his back and his ankles together. Then, again with the eagle's help, she hauled him onto the bed.

WHEN BOTAS OPENED his eyes, *Turandot* was playing in the living room. A bruise had come up on his temple and he appeared to be in a daze. Lucía, still naked, was sitting on the bed, contemplating him.

"Now," she said, "let's see if you can put two and two together."

Botas now saw that his legs and hands were tied. He looked at the woman.

"What's going on?" he said.

"Get your thinking cap on, and you'll see."

"What the hell did you hit me with?"

"With an eagle's foot. Starting to add up yet?"

"Look, what's your name? . . ."

"'My secret is hidden within me, / My name no one shall know, / On your mouth I will tell it / When the light shines.' Ring any bells?"

"Yes," said a bemused Botas.

She brought her lips right up to his, until they were all but touching.

"Turandot," she whispered. He still looked perplexed, and she added, "Lucía Turandot, in fact. My father was a Puccini fan. People call me Lucía."

Botas shook his head, as though this were all a dream and changing position might snap him out of it. It didn't.

"Look," he said, "the play was Roberta's idea—she's the producer—hers and Cáceres's together. They're a couple. But they told me they were going to talk to you, ask your permission. Did they not do that?"

"No."

"They even talked about emoluments for you, to reflect the fact the story belonged to you. . . ."

"Emoluments, such pretty words. Now I understand why you get so little work: You're so unconvincing."

"But I've done nothing to you!" he pleaded, trying to get free of his binds.

"You can't imagine all the things you've done to me, because for that you would need to have a bit of sensitivity. Here, listen to Pavarotti."

The music, coming in through the open living room door, brought tears to Lucía's eyes, as though it were playing on the other side of a wall.

"You destroyed my life," she said between tears. "People like you don't deserve anything, however cultured you may be."

Botas was still perplexed, incredulity etched on his face. Thunder clapped outside; the windows shook. Lucía went through into the living room, skipped the CD forward to "Nessun dorma," came back in, and joined in with Pavarotti's rendition. Botas was flabbergasted. Still naked, Lucía stood stroking the tattoo.

"Do you know how much it hurts getting a tattoo done here? It was a gift for you. Well, you already know all about that. Anything Roberta didn't tell you, Cáceres would have. A gift that you made a big joke of in the play, like the asshole you are."

"I'm sorry, Lucía," implored the actor.

"Do you know what the bird in the living room is called?"

Botas hesitated before deciding he was better off telling the truth.

"Calaf the Second. Roberta told me."

"Calaf the Second lives here now, but he's a descendent of the birds that flew around over the square in Peking with the impaled heads of Turandot's failed suitors. He's had a lot of practice in ripping off people's eyelids, plucking out their eyes. He's also expert at tearing people's tongues out."

"Lucía, please . . ."

"Now, you're going to do exactly as I say."

"Whatever you want."

Lucía went over to the man's clothes and hunted in the pockets for his cell phone.

"I thought about getting you to call Roberta, but I think we're better off sending a WhatsApp message. Tell me your PIN."

After unlocking the device, she sent a message to Roberta from Botas, urging her to come to the apartment and to be quick about it. Just as she expected, the reply came more or less immediately: "What's happening?"

Lucía replied: "It's a surprise, a really big one, something you can't even imagine. Drop whatever you're doing, jump in a cab, and come over. Not a word to Santiago."

"You've got it—I'm intrigued!"

Lucía then found Santiago Cáceres's contact and wrote him a similar message. She had to trust they would not arrive at exactly the same time.

"God," said Botas, "my head hurts."

"I'm not surprised; you've got a bruise the size

of an egg. If the music is bothering you, I'll turn it off."

"Oh, no, not at all," he said, for fear of opposing Lucía, who, for her part, had started to dress in anticipation of her new visitors.

ROBERTA ARRIVED FIRST, a look of surprise on her face as she entered the apartment, shooting Lucía a half-complicit, half-guilty smile.

"Go into the bedroom," said Lucía, nodding as if they were on the same side.

Roberta went to do so and, the moment she passed Lucía, was struck over the back of the head with a heavy object—an ornamental mortar made of copper, in her case. She fell wordlessly to the floor. A moment later, the doorbell rang—not the buzz of the downstairs entry phone; Cáceres must have found the door to the street open. Lucía hesitated for a moment and then went and let him in. Seeing Roberta lying on the floor, he stopped dead.

"She fainted," said Lucía.

The man crouched down next to the woman just as blood started to emerge from her scalp, and just as a cry came from Botas in the bedroom.

"Help!"

Cáceres, still crouching down, turned to Lucía with a quizzical look, at which she brought the mortar down on his skull. And despite the ferocity of the blow, the man tried to get to his feet. So Lucía hit him again, this time bringing a whitish substance to the surface of the bloody wound.

"It was a plover's head," she said to Calaf II, who had been looking on from his perch with a notable absence of opinion.

Cáceres was dead. Roberta was not. But Lucía solved that problem by going over and sinking her teeth into Roberta's throat, coming up with chunks of cartilage mixed with muscle and skin, all forming a homogenous paste in her mouth. Though the teeth she had used were her human ones, the technique of the throat rip was that of the eagle with its beak. There was now a gaping hole in Roberta's throat that left the brain stem visible.

"All yours," she said to the bird, which flapped down from the perch to peck at the gray mass oozing from the man's head before plunging its beak into the mess of Roberta's throat.

Lucía wiped her bloody mouth on her sleeve. She then swiveled her eagle's head and went on cleaning it on her plumage. Once she felt presentable once more, she returned to the bedroom. Botas gave her a questioning look as if to say, What just happened?

"What was written in the stars," she said, going and sitting on the side of the bed like someone visiting a convalescent. "It's time we had a talk."

"Whatever you want, Lucía. Whatever you say."

"And you're going to tell the truth. Maybe it's

something you've never done, maybe you're out of practice, but promise me that you'll try."

"I promise."

"Show me your tongue."

"What?"

"Stick your tongue out, dammit!"

Botas immediately did as he was told.

"More than that, you moron! Stick it out as far as you can."

The actor obeyed. Lucía scrutinized the tongue as though she were a doctor examining it.

"Have you never wondered why it's so pointed?"

"Honestly, no."

"Because it's a bird's tongue, moron. Look at mine."

Lucía stuck hers out so that he could see.

"Right . . ."

"You could have been the perfect bird man," she said, "but look what you've gone and done with your life instead."

Botas's bird eyes moved from side to side. He was trying to think fast. Perhaps he was wondering if there was some weak point of Lucía's that he might exploit. That was his only chance. But until some plan of action came to him, the best thing was to keep his mouth shut and not inflame the situation.

"You don't know what you need to say to get out of this, right?" said Lucía.

"I don't," he admitted.

"Why me?" she said. "Why did you choose me for that pantomime, that chance for all those people in the audience to have a good old laugh?"

"Your story interested me from the start, because it was real."

"What's that supposed to mean?"

"Real doesn't mean realistic. More than that, a real work of art should not be realistic. Reality and realism have nothing to do with each other, though most people get the two mixed up."

Lucía wasn't very clear about the difference, but it did feel to her as though Botas was telling the truth. She perceived that there was something in this, something of which he was possibly unaware, of deeper interest to him than what might be about to befall him.

"I've been in theater for many years," he said. "I'm a failed actor. I haven't failed out of a lack of talent, though, but, rather, an excess of it. I never had the opportunity to do something really big until you appeared. The only thing that interests me is reality."

"Well, there's a bit of reality on the living room floor that you're going to love."

"Ever since I was young," he continued, "I've been looking for a door that connects with reality, and you opened that door with the story of your life. I didn't steal it from you. I didn't steal your life; I went toward it with all the desperation of the shipwreck survivor spotting dry land."

"You're very convincing."

"I'm not trying to be. You told me to tell you the truth, and nothing closer to it occurs to me."

"Would you give your life for reality?" she asked.

"In an instant," he said.

"I'll make your wish come true; I'll give you a little reality in exchange for your liver. But first you have to give me something real, as well."

"Whatever you want."

Botas seemed suddenly to have entered a logic whereby he didn't mind being tied up. Something had shifted inside his head.

Lucía undressed again. She then doubled the pillow over so that the man's head was slightly elevated, and crouched over his face, offering him her genitals.

"Lick me with your bird's tongue," she said.

Botas obediently set about it. The physical genitals were Lucía's, but the metaphysical ones belonged to the eagle, so that, when the moment arrived, the woman and bird inhabiting the same space simultaneously experienced an orgasm, the intensity of which matched the storm raging outside. When Lucía got down, spent, and saw the actor's erection, she said, "Maybe you've been honest with me. Now for your slice of reality."

This said, she leaned down and took a tremendous, tearing bite out of his gut, beginning to eviscerate him as deftly as a vulture removing the insides of a dead deer. Botas gave a moan, somewhere between horror and pleasure, as his cock grew even more throbbingly erect. When the woman's mouth, guided by the eagle's clever beak, reached his liver, he gave the moan of a dying man and came, an arc of his semen shooting all the way to the ceiling.

At that moment, the entry phone buzzed. Lucía went back into the living room and, contemplating the scene before her, decided enough reality had now been created to compensate for the fictional hour and a half into which these three dead people had converted her life. She looked blankly at Calaf II, who was raking his beak around inside Cáceres's skull. Lucía flapped her wings out, loosening stiff muscles, and moved across the living room on her powerful eagle legs. When the entry phone buzzed again, she recalled the nonpassenger she had taken to the Canillas Police Station. It buzzed three more times. When it buzzed for the fourth time, she went over to the window, opened it, and threw herself out into the storm. She had barely flown two meters when her human, gravity-susceptible body fell away from that of the eagle, dropping like a stone, while the bird, free now of that burden, rose gloriously toward the place the rays of light were coming from.

Bellevue Literary Press is devoted to publishing literary fiction and nonfiction at the intersection of the arts and sciences because we believe that science and the humanities are natural companions for understanding the human experience. We feature exceptional literature that explores the nature of consciousness, embodiment, and the underpinnings of the social contract. With each book we publish, our goal is to foster a rich, interdisciplinary dialogue that will forge new tools for thinking and engaging with the world.

To support our press and its mission, and for our full catalogue of published titles, please visit us at blpress.org.

BELLEVUE LITERARY PRESS
New York